Coyote
Sunrise

୬୬

Nikki Broadwell

Airmid Publishing
Tucson Arizona

Airmid Publishing

This is a work of fiction. All names, characters, places and ideas presented here are the product of the author's imagination.

Formatting by: Rik Hall
(http://www.WildSeasFormatting.com)

1 4 1 2 2 0 1 5

Dedication

To all the people who care about animals and the world in which they roam.

"If you talk to the animals they will talk with you and you will know each other. If you do not talk to them you will not know them and what you do not know, you will fear. What one fears, one destroys." ~Chief Dan George, Tsleil-Waututh Nation, British Columbia, Canada~

Preface

I began this story after the Predator Masters hunting group arrived here in Tucson, Arizona. I protested with others about their practices, which are abhorrent to me. I am not against hunting, per se, but in my opinion trophy hunting for no other reason than to kill is despicable. I found out that the Fish and Game Department are not here to protect the animals; they are here to allow the indiscriminant killing of creatures who roam in our part of Arizona, mostly coyotes.

In 2015 there were resolutions passed by Pima County and the city of Tucson, but they only went as far as 'opposing any and all Predator Masters hunts'. However their 2016 convention is still listed on their website as taking place here. It is very difficult to find a way to ban them completely, but it is not impossible.

If you want to get involved or find out more about this issue, please contact
http://www.projectcoyote.org/
or
Greg Hale—Tucson Wildlife Advocates—
https://www.facebook.com/Tucson-Wildlife-Advocates-803878783041576/

1

"I do not understand humans! What the fuck is wrong with them?" Istaga's outrage echoed off the dark stone of the cave, reverberating in Sara's ears.

Lately his moods had been erratic and dangerous but she had to smile at his use of this particular swear word. Despite being a coyote he knew exactly how to place it in a sentence. Come to think of it, he didn't fully understand the concept of love or most human emotions but he was adept with swear words, as though his coyote nature understood them intuitively.

Sara and Istaga had been together nearly three years now. When she first met him he was hurt and vulnerable, showing up at her door in human form with a bullet lodged in his shoulder. *And I was the one who shot him,* she thought, remembering that night. As Istaga he had seemed foreign, but she would never have guessed how foreign he truly was. Their courtship, if you could call it that, had been filled with surprises, his animal magnetism impossible to resist. She had overlooked his oddness, chalking it up to the possibility that he had come up from South America and didn't understand much English or American mores. And their sexual connection was strong enough to override any possible misgivings she might have had.

She actually fainted the day he divulged who and what he was—after explaining it he demonstrated, switching from human to coyote and back again until all the blood drained from her head. But the strangeness of that was topped the day she turned into a coyote herself, loping after him into the desert and away from danger.

A shaman had bestowed his gift, but hers...it was an utter mystery how a normal woman could suddenly learn how to shift into an animal. Love and stress, she figured. Because if she hadn't shifted at that precise moment she would be in jail for a crime she didn't commit.

Sara's thoughts fled as Istaga followed his statement up with a growl that a normal human would not make, a sound she'd come to recognize as uniquely his.

"I only like being human when I'm with you," he answered, his narrowed yellow eyes focused on her. "The human species needs to be culled."

Culled, another word he'd recently picked up. Sara thought back to when she tried to teach him to read and the books she'd given him to help make sense of the human world. Some had been childhood stories like Charlotte's Web, a book she'd read to him early on, and Doctor Doolittle, the vet who could talk to animals. Simple stories but profound at the same time. But in the end she'd given up, figuring he would learn about humans from time spent with humans, not by information in books. He was uniquely himself and how he viewed things offered her another way of looking at life. "You're right about that," she said, meeting his gaze. "Now what brought up all this anger?"

"The hunters have arrived again, the ones who kill for sport, not for food."

Sara felt weak for a second and lowered to the floor to lean against the cave wall. "The group they call the predator masters?"

Istaga nodded, his eyes narrowing even further.

Sara stared at her mate, remembering the last time this happened. She'd known nothing about it until she and Istaga had come upon the area of slaughter. It had taken weeks to get over the sight of the dead and dying animals. Her trip to the Fish and Game Department had almost made matters worse. Despite her protestations they told her there was no law against it and no limit to it. Their impassive expressions made her sick.

Sara gazed at their two-year-old. "We need to be careful. We have Kaliska to consider now."

With the mention of her name Kaliska looked up from the array of strewn rocks on the cave floor. She gurgled and smiled, waving a piece of quartz in her baby fist.

"As much as I hate to say it, none of us are getting out of these human skins until after this hunt is over," Istaga announced, bending to pick up the baby. Kaliska let out a shriek of pleasure and promptly shifted into a coyote pup, wriggling out of his arms and running out of the cave.

When the pup stopped to look back, daring Istaga

to shift and chase her, Sara grabbed Istaga's arm. "How do we stop her from doing that?" she whispered.

Istaga watched the pup for a moment. "We cannot. That's why I'm worried. The hunters will be everywhere, Sara."

Outside the cave stars winked alive, silver blue between the dark tree branches and wheeling across the velvet dome, bringing an illusion of safety. Their secluded aerie lay between valley and sky and was hard to reach on foot, despite the gravel road below where the sound of cars occasionally reached their ears. The cave was one of several along this mountain ridge housing many species, predators and prey alike. There seemed to be a tacit agreement among them all to go further afield for their food, which was still plentiful. But if the balance was disturbed things could change. "I'm going to town tomorrow to talk with Rosie about it," Sara muttered before heading outside to retrieve her wayward baby.

It was late in the night when Istaga rolled over and took Sara in his arms. She didn't complain about being awakened, responding as she always did to his nips on her neck, his wandering hands that seemed to understand her body better than she did. He took her to places she'd never known, filled with imagery that caught at her senses making her believe in past lives. Sometimes in these visions they were animals, and sometimes humans, steeped in either the past or the future where life was not as it was here, but all of it was magical.

৵৵

Sara left the cave early the next morning, heading down the mountain in coyote form and then shifting as she drew closer to town. She ran her fingers through her short blonde hair registering how thick and gummy it was. She only noticed how desperately it needed washing when she came off the mountain to be in polite society. She laughed at herself for this way of looking at Black Base, a town on the fringes if there ever was one. Dirt roads, one bar, one café, a county building, a grocery store/post office, and a vet's office were nearly the only amenities. But it was a step up from living rough and being a coyote half the time.

In town she headed to the flat-roofed building that housed the county offices, heading up the steps to the glass door and pushing it open. It was lunchtime and the room was nearly empty, but Rosie still sat behind her desk, her gaze meeting Sara's over her computer screen.

"What's up?" her friend asked.

"They're back," Sara announced.

Rosie pursed her lips. "Look at this," she said, pulling up some info from the Internet. She turned the screen so Sara could see.

Spread across the screen was an advertisement that described the unlimited local hunting opportunities, the contests for the most kills. "Is there anything we can do about it?"

Rosie removed her close-up glasses and pushed her fingers through her curly dark hair. Half Hispanic and half African-American, her looks were exotic with her café au lait skin color and almond shaped brown eyes. Sara always felt frumpy around her, as though her blue eyes and blonde hair were ordinary and not very interesting.

"These hunts were outlawed back in 1998 but our illustrious governor at the time overrode it."

Sara frowned. "And our newly elected governor isn't any better. I hate that man and all the senators as well. They don't care about anything that matters! I've written but all they do is send some platitude-filled letter back that doesn't answer my questions. This is why I prefer life as a coyote." As these words tumbled out of her mouth Sara knew this was not entirely true. Lately she'd had longings to work on her computer and to drink beer in a pub and eat something besides meat and the occasional berry or nut. She was tiring of her life in the wild but hadn't yet admitted it to herself or to Istaga.

Rosie smiled. "I'm glad you came clean about your double life, Sara. I would have worried for years if you hadn't explained your disappearances." Her smile faded. "But I would suggest that you don't shift again until all of this business is done with."

Sara thought back to the day she broached the subject of shifting to Rosie. She'd tried to soften it but in the end she blurted out everything, not surprised by the look of shock on her friend's face. It had taken an hour or more before Rosie believed her and understood that Sara had fallen in love with a coyote. "We aren't planning to, but Kaliska—she's unpredictable."

"When do I get to meet that baby?"

"Maybe sooner than you think. How would you feel about putting us up for a few days? Kaliska needs to be corralled and if we're out on the land she could wander off. She's done it before and I would hate to have her picked up by one of these yahoos."

Rosie's expression was unsure but then she nodded. "My house is small but I'd love to have the company for a few days. But if I know you and Istaga, the two of you won't be around much. Am I right?"

Sara grinned but then her expression darkened. "We have to warn the animals and convince them to hide higher up in the mountains. The hunters have these calls they use that sound like coyotes in distress. The coyotes have to know so they don't get fooled."

"That doesn't sound easy. Didn't Istaga's pack shun him after he got so interested in humans?"

Sara nodded. "But there are lots of packs out there. You can't imagine how pissed off Istaga is right now."

Rosie stared into the distance. "I've seen him angry so I have a pretty good idea," she said.

Sara thought back to her early history with Istaga/Coyote and how he'd killed a man to save her. Afterward he'd been caught by animal control and taken to the local vet's office. Luckily Rosie worked for animal services and organized to have the rogue coyote relocated. "You know Rosie, if it wasn't for you he'd be dead."

"They were intent on euthanizing him. I'm just glad I did what I did. Weird to look back on that now since I had no idea who that coyote was, and I certainly didn't know you had a relationship with him."

Sara laughed. "Neither did I!" It had taken a few months before Sara realized that the man she'd fallen in love with was actually a shape shifter.

"And who could ever have guessed that you'd learn how to do it too?"

Sara shook her head and looked down. "I still wonder how that happened. I think it was love that did it."

Rosie looked skeptical. "I've loved many an animal, Sara, but I've never turned into any of them."

"I can't explain it. It just happened. But I was under tremendous stress at the time; maybe it was desperation that allowed it to happen. If I hadn't I'd have ended up back in Minnesota with Raleigh." She shuddered thinking of her husband, a nasty and self-serving man who would go to any lengths to keep her with him to help his political ambitions. So far she hadn't figured out how to get a divorce without having to face the man she hated most in the world.

"Never had the pleasure," Rosie said, making a face. "Does this mean I get to spend time alone with your baby?"

Sara smiled. "I'll go home and alert Istaga. If he agrees we'll be by early tomorrow."

❧

Istaga was crouched next to the fire pit when Sara entered, the fire sending flame shadows dancing across the dark stone of the cave, the smoke wending its way out the front. He looked up, his gaze bleak. "You won't believe what I found out."

One look at his expression told her it was something bad. "What is it?"

"Your former mate is a member of this hunting organization. He will be here this weekend.

Sara felt something squeeze her heart. "How did you find that out?"

Istaga gave a lopsided grin, revealing one of his canines. "I went to the bar in Black Base and talked to John."

When had he done that?

John and Sara were dating when she met Istaga. He was a nice enough guy who was also the town vet. It was John who had shot Istaga/Coyote with a tranquilizer gun after Coyote attacked and killed a man on the trail—in his defense, if Coyote hadn't come along at that moment Sara would be dead. But it was the news about Raleigh that made Sara's skin crawl. She'd hoped to never see or hear from him again. "Raleigh should be in jail. I guess if you have unlimited money you can buy your way out of just about anything, even murder."

Istaga stared at her blankly. He didn't fully understand the concept of money and what a huge part it played in American society. "John told me where the main hunts will be and how many hunters he thinks will come."

Sara met Istaga's gaze, noticing the animal-like gleam in his yellow eyes. At this moment he looked very dangerous. "Is John participating?"

"I do not think so."

"Is Kaliska sleeping?" Sara asked, heading deeper into the cave.

Istaga frowned. "I thought she was with you."

"I told you I was going into town. Don't tell me you left her here alone." Sara stared at him, unable to breathe. A second later both of them were calling and combing the cave. When they couldn't find her they ran outside, but after an hour of searching up and down the hill and along the ridge there was still no sign of her.

"I can't believe you took off and left her here!" Sara shouted, trying not to give way to panic. "Where could she be?"

Istaga's eyes narrowed and then he was Coyote, his mouth open in a snarl. Sara backed away and shifted, the two of them facing off with their hackles raised. It was Sara who lunged first, anger and frustration getting the better of her as she attacked her mate. The fight lasted barely a minute before they came to their senses and shifted into human form.

Istaga took hold of Sara's arm, making her face him. "It doesn't matter whose fault this is, only that Kaliska is missing and we have to find her."

Sara broke away from him, tears in her eyes. "Can you track her?"

"I didn't pick up her scent."

"What if a bobcat got her--or a mountain lion? Anything could have happened."

"How about a human?" Istaga asked, lifting his head and sniffing. A second later he was on all fours again, his nose to the ground.

"Wait!" Sara called, but he was already loping down the rocky hill. Sara tried to think but her mind refused to concentrate. When she left for town Istaga was in the cave. She'd assumed he would hang around, since she distinctly remembered telling him where she was going. How could he leave and not notice Kaliska?

Whoever or whatever had taken the baby was long-gone by now. And if it was a human and the baby had been in pup form there was no telling what would happen. But worse than that, if it was a mountain lion, Kaliska was surely dead.

Sara shifted and followed Coyote down the hill. After swimming across the narrow river at the bottom she headed into a thicket of bushes and spindly trees, but in the muddled aromas of vegetation she lost him. Her coyote mind worked on instinct but right now she needed logic. A second later she was herself again and frantic with worry as she headed for the road.

Sara jumped when a truck backfired, all her senses on alert. A series of coyote yips and then a howl split the silence, Istaga's unmistakable distress call. She pushed her way through the thick bushes and took off running.

2

$\mathcal{T}$he truck disappeared in a cloud of dust, leaving Coyote behind. He howled in frustration and then turned when he heard Sara call. She was shrieking words he didn't understand. He shifted, opening his arms to embrace the sun-haired woman who made his heart sing. "I heard her," he mumbled, his words lost in her tangled, sage-scented hair. For a moment he forgot everything, the scent and feel of her blocking out all thought.

She pulled away her eyes wide and frightened. "Is it Raleigh?"

He came back to the present, his eyes narrowing as he remembered the truck and the sound of his pup. "I couldn't see the driver."

"Human or coyote call?"

"Coyote but who knows how long she'll stay that way?"

"She has a much better chance as a human, Istaga. At least she might be taken to a shelter or child services."

"If someone took her on purpose why would they take her to a shelter?"

"If I found a baby alone in a cave I'd take her to a shelter."

"What if she was a pup when he found her? It

could be a hunter. I'm going after him."

Coyote felt a dread he'd never experienced. His animal mind worked in different ways and he knew if he caught up with the man driving that truck he would kill him. And he also knew that if he did that Sara would be very upset. Within his muddled brain the two sides of him fought, but in the end it was the animal that won out. The wind whispered the answer. He would find his pup and dispatch the man who took her.

Sara felt helpless and out of control as she hurried after her mate. The roar of trucks and jeeps was loud in her ears—hunters ripping across the darkening desert in search of nocturnal animals. When shots rang out she crouched in the weeds next to the road. She heard the distress call of a coyote but it was one she didn't recognize. And then she realized that it was exactly what Istaga had told her about—a call that the hunters used. She felt physically sick for a second. A truck came toward her; its headlights blinded her for a second before she heard the screech of brakes as the vehicle rolled to a stop next to her.

"Are you lost, little lady?" the gray-haired driver asked, looking her over with a puzzled expression.

Sara glanced down at the ragged denim shirt that came to her knees, the one she always seemed to be wearing when she shifted-- another mystery she hadn't solved. At least she wasn't naked. "Can you give me a lift into town?"

"Sure can. Hop in."

Sara opened the passenger door and slid onto the worn seat. She slammed the door closed and turned to the driver. "Are you one of the hunters who just came into town?"

He put the car into gear and let out the clutch. "I'm a hunter but I don't belong to that organization."

Sara let out a long sigh, her gaze moving down the dusty road ahead of them. "Do you approve of what they do?"

"I eat what I kill," he said, without taking his eyes off the road.

The disdain in his tone encouraged Sara to continue her questions. "I think that's the way it should be. I hate the idea of killing for no reason." They were close to town now and out of the corner of her eye she saw a coyote moving through the brush on the side of the road. Istaga. "Before you picked me up a truck went by. I think it was red. Do you have any idea who it belongs to?"

The man turned. "I've seen it before but I don't know who it belongs to. I do know he's one of 'em."

"Where might I find him?" Sara tried to keep her features neutral but there was something boiling inside her that wanted to get out. If she'd been a coyote she would have howled loud enough to wake the dead.

"He and the rest of the group stay at the Red Lion, just down the road. I'll drop you there if you like."

"Thank you. I just want to talk to him for a minute."

"Don't expect to talk any sense into those people.

Believe me, I've tried. They make regular hunters look bad, you know? And they kill off all the predators and upset the balance."

Sara opened her mouth and closed it, afraid of what might spew out if she allowed herself to speak. Right now it was taking every bit of her will power to keep control.

A few minutes later they rolled into the parking lot and he stopped the truck. "Be careful with these people. They don't think like the rest of us."

Sara tried to smile but failed miserably. "Thanks for the lift," she said, opening the door and sliding out.

She searched the parking lot for the red truck but couldn't find it. Finally she left the Red Lion and headed back the way she'd come, hoping to catch up with Istaga. He was good at tracking and would surely have found a way to stay on the scent.

It was close to midnight before she found her mate, coming upon him suddenly along a lonely stretch of road. The hunters were gone now and the lack of night calls from the local coyotes chilled her to the core.

Istaga shifted when he saw her and jogged toward her. "I lost him."

"He's staying at the Red Lion but his truck wasn't there when I searched." And then she noticed the cuts along Istaga's cheekbone. She placed her fingers gently on his face, tracing the line of red. "What happened?"

"I tried to jump into the back of the truck but I missed." He rubbed a hand across his face, wincing.

"Are you sure he has Kaliska?"

Istaga's eyes turned dark. "He has her all right. He

locked her inside some box in the back of his truck. I heard her whining."

A sharp pain went through Sara's stomach. "What do we do now?"

"We go back to the Red Lion and wait for him. He has to sleep sometime."

∞᷄ঌ

Istaga didn't want to scare Sara but he was afraid of what they might find when they reached that truck. There couldn't be much air inside that small space and when he heard Kaliska's plaintive whines they sounded weak.

By the time they reached the Red Lion parking lot the red truck was parked, but when they opened the compartment in back there was no sign of Kaliska. Istaga sniffed and turned to Sara. "She was so scared she let go of her water."

He picked up a rock and broke the window on the passenger side, setting off the car alarm. After that he grabbed Sara's hand and pulled her into the tall weeds between the road and the motel.

"How did you know about the alarm?" she whispered.

"The noise? I've been around these smoke spewing beasts enough to know a few things."

A few minutes later a man arrived, his face dark with anger. He scanned the parking lot and then used his key to turn off the alarm. "Goddammit," he muttered, examining the glass.

When Sara lunged toward him Istaga put his hand

over her mouth and pulled her further out of sight. "I'm going to follow him," Istaga hissed into her ear. "Stay here."

"But it's Raleigh..."

"If he has her I'll get her back."

Istaga took off across the parking lot, hiding behind cars as he went. When Raleigh reached a door, Istaga waited until he was inside before pursuing him. He heard a baby's cry and then heard Raleigh yell, "Shut up you little freak!"

A loud wail followed and then a whine that could only be coyote.

"Jesus Christ! What in hell are you? You've got to be worth some money to some scientist somewhere. I just hope you don't die on me. What the hell do you eat, anyway?"

A moment later Raleigh let out a yell of pain. Apparently Kaliska had bitten him. And a second after that Istaga kicked the door open. Raleigh had his back turned trying to wash the blood off his hand and the startled expression in his eyes made Istaga smile. But that expression was nothing compared to the look on the man's face when Istaga shifted, picked the pup up in his mouth and ran out the door.

Istaga was halfway across the parking lot when he heard the report from the gun. A burning pain went through his back and leg. He kept on running, his only thought to get the baby to Sara and safety. But when he reached the place where he'd left Sara she was gone.

A second after that he heard Sara scream and turned to see Raleigh with his arm tight around her middle. Sara wriggled to get away but he was a big man.

"This is a night to be remembered," Raleigh snorted. "First that abomination and now you. Is that your baby, Sara? Because if it is you're even weirder than I thought. It should be in a zoo or in some kind of freak show. And what's with that freaking coyote? He's been shot, you know. Is he one of your pets?"

Istaga dropped Kaliska in the weeds and then growled at her to stay put. A second later he leapt from his hiding place, his jaws open in a snarl of fury. The gun went off but the shot went wild as Raleigh whirled and let go of Sara. By that time Istaga was at his throat and Raleigh was screaming at the top of his lungs.

"Don't kill him!" Sara shouted, pulling on Coyote's tail.

Istaga was dimly aware of what he was doing. He knew there was a reason why he needed to end this man's life but hearing her voice stopped him.

"Come on, Istaga. We have to get out of here before we're seen!"

Coyote was intent on completing what he started, the thought of it singing in his blood, but he couldn't ignore her. He left the man on the ground and followed her, gratified to hear the low moans of pain, the gurgle of blood as it filled the man's throat from the wound he'd inflicted. Maybe he would die.

"Shift!" he heard her yell. She was ahead of him and he watched her pick up the coyote pup and hug her to her chest before sprinting across the street. He knew what that word meant, was on two feet a second later, narrowly missing being hit by a car in his confused and injured state. Sirens whined in his ears as he ran across the field on the other side of the road. By the time they reached the end of the field they were coyotes again, nimbly jumping the fence to disappear into the shadows on the other side.

3

They'd made it back to the cave to hide out and sleep, but now the day was nearly done and Sara had the chance to look him over more closely. "We may have to take you to the hospital," Sara said, examining the gunshot wounds. He had several deep oozing lacerations on his upper back and thigh.

"Animal doctor would be a better choice."

"If I took you to the vet in your coyote form they'd relocate you to Utah in a second. Either that or you'd be euthanized."

"What does that mean?"

"It means dead, Istaga. If I know Raleigh the news is full of what happened last night. And now that he knows I'm involved he'll have someone tracking us for sure."

"If he lived." Istaga looked hopeful as he turned his head to stare up at her out of his yellow eyes.

"You didn't kill him." Sara pressed white sage onto his back where the pellets had dug into the flesh. She had tried unsuccessfully to remove them the night before and hoped the herb would help bring the buckshot closer to the surface. "You're lucky the other shot just grazed your leg. That could have been really bad."

Istaga pushed himself up to sit next to her. "My

back feels better."

"If I can't get those pieces of metal out by tomorrow I'm taking you to the doctor."

"What about Toh Yah? He could help."

Sara pictured the kind face of the Navajo man who had helped them in the past. "He's hours from here and with your leg the way it is I doubt you could make it."

"I say we head up into the hills. It's what we planned to begin with."

The idea of heading even further away from civilization had been Istaga's idea, not hers. She'd only agreed because of how adamant he'd been. Sara turned to see where Kaliska had gone before answering. "Kaliska is still weak and that's too long a trip for her."

Istaga's gaze went outside where their daughter played in the waning light. He let out a growl that made Sara's skin prickle. "She could have died in that box. I wish you hadn't stopped me."

"Killing is not the answer. You know that." When Sara's gaze met Istaga's the feral look on his face made her shiver. He was animal and she'd observed his wildness many times, but this expression struck her as new. Protecting their baby had brought out a primal part of him she'd never seen before.

"It is when it comes to our baby, especially when it's the man who kept you prisoner and framed you for murder."

Sara was surprised how much Istaga understood about the workings of the human world. He might not understand the concept of money but he certainly got the idea of how humans preyed on each other in ways alien to coyotes. "I don't want his blood on my hands. I couldn't deal with it. Let's just be grateful that we have our baby back. Now we have to figure out how to keep the cops from catching up with us."

"And keep these hunters from laying waste to all predators," Istaga muttered before standing.

Sara watched him limp away into the trees where he went to relieve himself. "Come in now, Kaliska. It's time to sleep," she urged, gesturing to the baby. But before she could grab her Kaliska had shifted and run after Istaga. "Kaliska, come back!"

"I've got her," Istaga called a moment later.

Both of them had been keeping a close eye on the baby, but it was proving to be difficult. Kaliska's frequent shifts happened at odd times when no one was expecting it and kept Sara and Istaga off balance. They had to instill some control if they were to keep her safe.

❧

After two days of treating his back with white sage and hot compresses, Sara could only manage to dig out a few more pellets. Istaga was not able to hunt and his mood was decidedly irritable. The wound was festering already, an angry red that was hot to the touch. "You have to go to a doctor," she insisted. "The wound is infected. You need antibiotics."

Istaga stared at her blankly. "It is better," he said, twisting around to look at it.

"It's not better, it's worse. We have to go to town. I'll ask Rosie where we should go."

After arguing with her for a few minutes Istaga finally gave in, a sure sign he was in pain.

Because of Istaga's wounds it took over two hours to reach the county building where Rosie worked. Once they were close enough Sara handed over the baby and told him to hide. "I'll be right back."

Rosie was behind her desk when Sara came through the door, a look of worry appearing on her face. "What are you doing here?" she whispered, looking around.

"Istaga got shot and I need to take him to a doctor, but I don't think we should go to the hospital."

Rosie stood and came around the desk. "Sara, what happened the other night is all over the news. You'd better take my truck and drive into Sarita. There's a tiny clinic there and hopefully they haven't been watching the national news." Rosie reached into her jeans pocket and handed her a set of keys. "Be careful. The police are looking for you two."

"What are they saying?" Sara whispered.

"They're saying that some enormous coyote attacked a man at the Red Lion and nearly killed him. The other stuff borders on surreal. Some guy filmed it all."

"You mean the...?"

Rosie nodded. "The shifting and all of it. People are freaking out about shape shifters coming to steal their children."

"Oh my god."

"And Raleigh is doing everything in his power to mobilize the police to go after you. Not only are you implicated in the death of his lawyer friend, but also now you're mixed up in bestiality. According to him you're a freak of nature and so is your baby."

Sara laughed even though her throat had nearly closed up. "I was sure all that was forgotten by now. He's the bastard who killed his friend, not me. What about Istaga? Isn't he a freak too?"

Rosie grabbed her arm. "This isn't funny. The cops and god knows who else are looking for you."

Sara met her friend's worried gaze. "Raleigh's vigilante friends are after us too? Is Sarita far enough?"

"I certainly hope so. It will take an hour and a half to get there and the town is tiny. With any luck at all they are blissfully unaware of shape shifters roaming around and attacking humans."

Sara gave her friend a quick hug before hurrying back to where she'd left Istaga and Kaliska. "The cops and Raleigh and all his coyote-hunting friends are searching for us. We have to be super careful."

"I figured as much," he said, picking up Kaliska and following her to Rosie's truck.

❦

They were on the highway when she finally admitted everything Rosie told her. "Someone recorded the entire thing on their cell phone, Istaga. There's footage of us shifting!"

Istaga looked confused, his gaze sliding sideways. "I don't understand."

"You know what a cell phone is, right? Well, you can take pictures with it as well as call people. Someone used it to take a moving picture of us turning into coyotes and you attacking Raleigh."

"I knew I should have killed him," Istaga muttered.

Sara shook her head. "That would have been way worse!" When Kaliska climbed out of Istaga's arms and crawled toward Sara's lap she pushed the baby back. "Can you hang on to her? We're almost there. I think she's hungry."

When Istaga reached for the baby, Kaliska began to cry and nothing either of them did or said could stop her. By the time Sara found the clinic Kaliska was red-faced and nearly hysterical. She pulled the truck over and unbuttoned her shirt. "I have to feed her before we go in." When she glanced toward Istaga he was slumped down in the seat with his eyes closed. She pulled the baby into her lap, trying to let go of her anxiety. It would sour her milk.

Ten minutes later Kaliska was happy again, chortling and playing with the dice hanging from the rear-view mirror. "Istaga? Are you okay?"

Istaga opened one eye. "My body feels hot and cold at the same time."

Sara reached over to feel his forehead. "You have a fever. Come on, let's get inside and get those pellets out of your back."

"What will you tell them?"

Sara thought for a moment. "I'll say you were hunting and a friend of yours mistook you for a coyote."

"Very funny."

"Well? It could be true you know. I just hope they

haven't been watching the news." Sara reached for Kaliska and opened the door. By the time she got around to the other side Istaga was standing unsteadily next to the truck. She shifted the baby to her hip and looped an arm through his, helping him up the steps and into the small brick building.

Inside there was a television going with news clips that featured her and Istaga. She cringed as she watched the scene in the parking lot—even with the sound off it was horrible to see Istaga as Coyote, teeth bared as he jumped on Raleigh. But when she looked around the small room she realized there were only a couple of waiting patients and they were not paying attention to the television. She hurried to the desk and told the nurse who she was and why she was there, reaching into her bag to grab her insurance card. "He doesn't speak a lot of English," she told the nurse, glancing at Istaga who looked about to pass out.

"And what is the nature of the injury?"

"His friend accidentally shot him."

The nurse laughed. "Happens more often than you'd think. Go on back. You can fill in his information after the doc sees him," she added, with a worried glance at Istaga's beet red, sweaty face.

By the time the doc had fixed him up Istaga had turned into a snarling replica of himself. It had been all Sara could do to keep him from shifting and biting the doctor while the poor man was cleaning out his wound and stitching it up. The leg wound was easier but Sara was very relieved once it was over.

Meanwhile Kaliska had been in the middle of things, getting in the way and needing to be restrained on more than one occasion. Sara had been terrified she would suddenly shift. But surprisingly the baby had remained human for the entire time. If Sara had known how nerve-wracking this would be...

"He'll need to be on antibiotics," the young doc told her, glancing warily at the dark-haired man who had an expression on his face that even scared Sara. "Don't let him go back to Mexico and forget to take them along. He should have come in right after this happened." He handed her a bottle of pills. "And give him one of these for the pain. Every six hours if it persists." He pulled open a drawer and grabbed a few packets and stuffed them into a bottle.

"I'll make sure," she answered, reaching for the pills. "Thanks so much."

"Wait!" the nurse called out as they were hurrying toward the door. "You need to fill in the form!"

When Istaga turned his narrowed yellow eyes toward her she blanched, her hand going to her throat. "Never mind. I have your address and insurance information." She smiled weakly.

In the truck Istaga let out the howl he'd been holding in.

"Take these," Sara said, handing him her water bottle and holding out an antibiotic and a pain pill.

He choked them down and turned to her. "Do not make me do this again," he growled.

For a moment she saw the coyote in his face, as

though he'd partially shifted, but a second later he was Istaga. "Don't get shot again," she replied, turning the key in the ignition.

The truck roared to life and she eased away from the clinic, a feeling of immense relief dropping her shoulders to their proper place. They could have been discovered as the shape shifters in the parking lot, Kaliska could have shifted, Istaga could have attacked the doc—it was miracle they made it through the appointment without some sort of mishap. She glanced at Kaliska on Istaga's lap, her thumb in her mouth. When had she learned to suck her thumb?

Once she was on the highway she glanced over, not surprised to see that Istaga was asleep. His head lolled against the seat, dark strands of hair tangled around his face. Kaliska was curled up in his lap with her head on his chest, his arm wrapped around her. She felt a wave of love for both of them, her heart full as she pulled her attention back to the road.

By the time they reached Rosie's work Istaga was out of sorts and volatile, threatening to turn into Coyote and take off with their baby. He had already made her pull over twice to throw up in the weeds, his face growing paler and paler. She wasn't sure what had caused the change, but it frightened her. She left him in the truck and went to return the keys.

"What kind of pills did you say the doc gave you?" Rosie asked after she described what was going on.

"Only antibiotics. Oh, and a pain killer."

"What kind of pain killer, Sara? If it's Percocet or Vicodin those could be lethal to a coyote. They're really strong and have been known to cause what you're describing."

Sara stared at her friend. "What do I do? He's already taken it."

"Just don't give him any more. Do you guys want to stay with me for a couple of days? If he's feeling sick it might be better than staying in a cave."

Sara glanced out the window, trying to catch sight of Istaga, but he was no longer sitting in the truck. "I don't think he'd agree to it. He's anti-humans right now with this hunt going on and Raleigh."

Rosie pressed her lips together. "I don't blame him."

Sara gave Rosie a quick hug before she went to look for Istaga. She searched in the weeds and up and down the street but there was no sign of them. After calling for several minutes she hurried back inside. "Istaga and Kaliska are gone."

Rosie looked up from her computer screen. "He probably got tired of waiting. You'll find both of them back at the cave."

"I hope so."

∾⌇∾

It took Sara longer than she'd planned to get back to their refuge up in the mountains. On her way out of town she'd spied Raleigh's red truck at the gas station and had to circle around to avoid him. There were more cop cars cruising around than usual, another reason why she had to lay low.

Once she was away from town she shifted, knowing it would take less time on four legs. The moon was up, spreading silver light across the pale desert landscape and seeming to light her way. Her belly was empty and she was anxious to see her pup and her mate, but other than that her mind was on the pungent scents riding the cool night air and the other animals roaming and trying to stay out of sight. In the distance she heard sirens, a sound that never failed to make her heart beat faster.

Her anxiety began to taper once she reached the river and swam across. There was no light from the fire when she worked her way up the steep cliff face toward their cave. Her coyote mind pictured raw meat instead of cooked, her mouth filling with saliva. But as she approached the cave she stopped to listen. There were no sounds coming from within. Before she processed the thought she was standing on two legs, alarm filling her body with adrenaline. Ducking her head under the overhanging lip of the cave she entered dark space. There was no one there.

4

*W*hen Sara heard rustling in the bushes she went into a panic. She was just hiding when Coyote appeared, Kaliska trailing behind him. He shifted immediately and came close to take her in his arms. "I'm glad you're back," he whispered.

When he kissed her Sara relaxed against him, feeling the physical desire that always welled up when she was around him. What finally pulled them apart was the whine from the coyote pup followed by a very annoyed baby who pushed herself up on two legs and toddled toward them. Sara bent to pick her up and then kissed her hair, her face, and her neck. "My sweet one. When you weren't here I..." her voice trailed off when she met Istaga's gaze. His eyes, usually full of light, were dark with anger, his mouth a thin line. "What's wrong?" Sara asked.

"The hunters were here while we were gone. Have you been inside?"

"Just for a minute, but when you weren't here I..."

"Raleigh must have given them directions. I heard them coming and took Kaliska into the woods up on the hill." He pointed to the pines that lined the ridge. "They were down here cursing and throwing shit around."

Istaga led the way into the cave and Sara followed,

surprised to see all their belongings strewn across the floor. Moonlight shone on her two aluminum pots that were now dented. She picked up her toothbrush, trying to remove the grit and then noticed her clothing that had been stepped on and dragged through the dirt. The oatmeal, pabulum and fruit she'd bought at the market had been emptied from their containers, joining the rest of the mess.

Sara shook her head. "I guess we'd better move on." She found one of several candles pulled out of their box and then crawled on her hands and knees to find the matches. After lighting it she set it into a holder and placed it on a small jutting rock too high for Kaliska to reach.

Sara lowered herself to the floor, pulled the baby close and unbuttoned her shirt, glad to have something to do besides think about what had happened here. Kaliska curled against her, taking the breast. She watched Istaga pace, his dark eyebrows pulled together. A few minutes later he hurried outside and she heard him retching. "Istaga, did you take another pill?" she called. He didn't answer.

By the time he came inside again Kaliska was playing with the yellow coyote gourd filled with seeds. The baby made a happy gurgle, her grubby hand swinging the gourd by the small stem at its top, the seeds making a swishing sound as they moved from side to side. When she let it go, it banged against the cave wall and then split apart, seeds flying everywhere.

Sara had learned that the pulp of these gourds was used to make soap and had used it a couple of times when she ran out of whatever she'd brought from town. But this one was dried, the pulp gone. Kaliska crawled toward the broken gourd and picked up one half of it. When the baby turned, her face was contorted into the expression that always came just before she cried. But before all hell broke loose Istaga was there with another gourd. Kaliska grabbed it out of his hands, her expression changing to a smile of delight.

Sara gathered their things together and stuffed everything she could fit into her backpack. "You didn't answer me about those pills. Did you take another? Rosie said they're probably bad for you."

Istaga crouched next to her. "I took one for pain because I hurt."

"Don't take any more. That's why you're throwing up."

"Better bringing up the contents of my stomach than not being able to walk."

Sara shook her head, trying to ignore his odd logic. "Where are they?"

"I left them in the woods before we shifted." He eyed her bulging pack. "What are you doing?"

"Do you plan to stay here after what happened?"

"It is too late to start now. We can go when the sun rises again."

Sara nodded, realizing the toll his injury had taken. He needed to sleep.

Istaga disappeared into the bushes for a moment and when he reappeared he was holding a rifle and the two pill bottles.

Sara stared in horror at the weapon. "Where did

you get that?"

"While they were ransacking our home Kaliska and I snuck down and took it out of their truck."

"I don't like this, Istaga. I don't feel comfortable with you having a weapon. If we need to shift what will you do with it?"

"I'll leave it at the place we settle. I don't feel safe without some sort of defense. These people are loco."

Sara thought about what Rosie had said and her own experience on the way out of town. Raleigh had already discovered where they lived. It wouldn't be long before he brought the cops up here. They would have to leave at first light.

❦

It was not yet dawn when Istaga took the baby, papoose style, on his back and headed into the forest. Sara followed, carrying the backpack bulging with everything she could fit in.

He led the way up a narrow animal trail, barely pausing when they reached the higher ridge. He seemed better after getting some rest and foregoing the pain pill. Before they left the cave she'd forced another antibiotic on him and insisted that he eat some of the trail mix she'd managed to save from their stores.

Before the sun was at its zenith they'd climbed into the peaks where the big horn sheep roamed. The valleys here were filled with springs, the ridges covered in ponderosa, Arizona pine trees and aspen. Game and water would be plentiful, but getting to town would not be easy.

Another few hours of walking brought them even further into wilderness. Sara wondered about the dangers up here from the big cats, but she was too exhausted to say anything. And to be honest the lions didn't scare her as much as Raleigh and his posse of crazies. She sat on a rock and watched Istaga scouting around for a viable cave. When he gestured, she followed him up a small hill to an opening that faced east. They made a fire and ate the nuts and dried fruits she'd brought along. Neither one had the strength to hunt. Once dinner was over and Sara had arranged their belongings inside the cave she took the baby in her arms and curled up to go to sleep.

❧

Sun streamed into the cave, waking Sara with its intensity. For a long moment she wasn't sure where she was and then the memory of the long day before entered her mind. She sat up and looked around, noticing that this cave was much deeper than their former one. Perhaps it had another exit, which would surely help in times of danger. Istaga sat cross-legged outside the opening his black hair glossy in the sun. Somewhere close the baby prattled away in her secret language.

When she ducked outside Istaga smiled, the first expression of this nature she'd seen on his face for several weeks. "Did you sleep?" she asked, moving next to him.

"A little. I don't need as much as you do."

That was true enough. He never seemed to sleep

for long and his stamina was three times what hers was. "How is your back?"

Istaga took off his shirt and turned so she could see his wound. It was still red but the swelling was gone and it was no longer infected. "Looks good," she said. "Did you take an antibiotic this morning?"

Istaga shook his head. "Give me one," he asked, holding out his hand.

She went into the cave and grabbed the bottle from where she'd stashed it and handed him a tablet. "Did she eat?" she asked, watching her baby play.

"We caught a squirrel earlier. I didn't save you any," he added, looking worried for a moment.

"You ate it raw?"

He nodded, looking guilty. "Kaliska hunted with me."

Her two-year-old had caught a squirrel?

"She's good at it, Sara," he continued. "This was her first kill."

Sara felt ill for a moment but then she remembered that she had also killed rabbits and squirrels as well as rats and mice, and had eaten many of them raw. "You feel safe here, it seems."

"I do. We're high enough up and in a wilderness area. I suspect there's no hunting allowed, but I could be wrong."

"What about mountain lions?"

"Unless there's a shortage of game we'll be safe."

"Kaliska?"

"We'll keep a close eye on her. And this cave is deep--safer than our other one. Are you hungry?"

Sara noticed the rumbling in her stomach. "I think I am."

"I'll find you something. Start the fire."

While he was gone Sara set to work finding twigs and branches to make a fire. She could hear a stream gurgling not far down the hill and went to investigate, carrying the baby and a pot along with her. The baby seemed entranced with the reflections and the little stones on the bottom of the pool and it took a lot of cajoling to get her back up the hill.

❧

Sara had the fire going and was contentedly feeding the baby by the time Coyote returned. He shifted and retrieved his knife from the cave and then set to work on the rabbit. When he finished skinning it he pushed a sharpened stick through the body and set it over the flames. Once Kaliska was fed Sara turned to the meat like a starving animal. She couldn't remember her last meal.

The baby was asleep when Istaga came to her. It was the first time since his injury that he'd been well enough and the expression on his face made her pulse quicken. She glanced at the sleeping child whose naps lasted an hour or more, and then followed him deeper inside the cave. Their bodies fit together perfectly. She couldn't get enough of him.

❧

As the halcyon days went by, pleasant and warm, Sara found herself growing restless. It had been over two months and although she felt safe there was something gnawing at her. She had taken to walking into the mountains, exploring the valleys and the pools of water collecting from the springs. Sometimes she brought Kaliska along, bathing with her in the cool water and letting the baby paddle around. Other times she left her with Istaga who was happy to take her on his daily hunts. As a coyote Kaliska was nearly full grown, but Sara did not want to give up the special bond that she and the human baby still shared.

Sara often thought about Rosie and missed the benefits of being close to town. There was good coffee, wine and beer, not to mention conversation and laughter with her own kind. She even missed her electronic devices and shopping for skin creams and silly things like make-up. Up here her lips were chapped, her skin dry as well. She tried to stay out of the direct sun but her face burned nonetheless. She had no mirror, no lip balm and no sunscreen. There was also no signal for her phone and the battery had long since died. Istaga was not much of a conversationalist and when he did say something it was mostly practical and had to do with plans for the day or hunting. There was no idle chitchat and no banter. The sex was good but without some deeper conversation even that was growing old. She loved him but the novelty of life in the wild was wearing off. She was not a coyote.

Istaga seemed completely contented with their life and had laughingly spoken about bringing another 'half breed' into the world. It wasn't lack of trying on his part that kept Sara from conceiving, but for her part she was relieved it hadn't happened. Maybe the breastfeeding was keeping her in a state of infertility. If that were the case she'd keep it up as long as she could—it was hard enough taking care of one shifter. Istaga was not the domestic type and when he did take care of Kaliska it was to take her hunting.

On the flip side they were safe up here and maybe the hullabaloo caused by the person who recorded the scene at the Red Lion had died down by now.

With Istaga's tutelage Kaliska was learning about being a coyote, but Sara thought she should also have the chance to be around humans and play with other children. She tried to put her mind on other things but as the days and weeks went by Sara began to feel an urgency to go back. Surely by now the hunters had moved on and Raleigh had gone home to Minnesota. And Rosie must be frantic with worry. When she brought it up to Istaga his expression turned stony.

"I'm not talking about moving back there," she explained. "I just need to see my friends and be with humans and do human things for a while."

"I'm human. Kaliska's human. What more do you need?" Istaga's unsmiling yellow eyes regarded her coldly. He pushed his hair back from his face with both hands in a gesture of impatience. "I've stayed in human form because of you."

"You become Coyote every day to go hunting. I would hardly say you've sacrificed because of me. And what about the other benefits that you obviously enjoy?" She kept his gaze, refusing to back down, but when he wouldn't look away she finally had to break the connection. His narrowed animal look of fury was too much for her. "Istaga, I know you don't understand what I'm trying to tell you. Our baby needs to be around humans her own age."

Istaga laughed. "And what happens when she shifts? I see nothing but trouble if you take her back there."

Sara glanced outside where Kaliska played. "She's old enough to control it. We just need to impress upon her how important it is."

Istaga shook his head and turned away. "Do what you want, Sara, but do not expect me to wait around."

Sara placed her hand on his shoulder. "I only want to visit for a little while."

Istaga shook her hand loose. A split second later he was Coyote and gone before she could say another word. Kaliska shifted as he ran by and was about to head after him when Sara grabbed her. "You stay here with me," Sara said firmly, holding the pup by the scruff of her neck.

❧❦

Istaga did not return that night or the one after that and on the morning of the third day Sara had made up her mind. She packed a few things and hoisted Kaliska onto her back. "We're going on a trip," she told her before heading down the mountain.

5

*R*osie eyes went wide as Sara came through the door with Kaliska on her hip. The oversized sunglasses and scarf Sara purchased at the gas station did not fool her friend. "I'll just be a second," she said, turning back to her computer.

A few minutes later she rose from her desk and gave Sara a long hug. "I was worried," she whispered. "We need to talk."

"What's going on?" Sara asked once they were out of earshot.

Rosie frowned. "Come on, girl. Don't tell me you don't know! That cell phone recording has gone viral. It's all over the Internet."

Sara stared at her friend in horror. "I thought it would have died down by now!"

"Most think it's special effects but Raleigh has a different story to tell. An ambulance took him to the hospital to be treated for bite wounds. They were pretty bad. According to the news he's had a series of rabies shots and a couple of rounds of strong antibiotics."

"But it's been months now! What's he saying?" Sara whispered.

"He's saying that the baby is a freak of nature and that his former wife, a woman wanted by the police for murder, is having sex with an animal and is involved in some kind of experimental breeding program between animals and humans. He described it as seriously fucked up, his words, not mine. He's pretty convincing."

Sara stared into the dry weeds and cactus that lay alongside the building. The morning sun was low and limning the edges of the prickly pears in an aura of gold. When she turned back to Rosie she saw the worry in her friend's brown eyes. The woman was truly beautiful, something she hadn't taken in before. Rosie had become her best friend, her *only* friend, and the one person who knew the truth and supported her unconditionally.

"Sara? Are you all right?"

"I'm not sure," she said, moving to sit down on the concrete steps. The baby let out a cry and she absentmindedly unbuttoned her shirt, giving her the breast.

Rosie sat down beside her and put an arm around her shoulders. "We can deal with this. You and Istaga have friends on the rez who know what you are. Maybe you guys should take a trip up to Page —give things a chance to calm down."

"It's been over two months. If they haven't calmed down by now I doubt they will. The reason I came down is because Istaga and I had a fight and he took off." She paused to move the baby to the other breast and continued. "He wishes he'd killed Raleigh that night."

Rosie looked away. "It might have been better if he had. That way Raleigh wouldn't be talking to the press every day and any onlookers would have thought they were hallucinating."

Sara looked down at the baby who was now playing with her belt buckle. She buttoned her shirt and put Kaliska on the ground, watching her toddle toward Rosie. "I can't live out there anymore. It's just too far away. It took me nearly three days to get here and I was traveling fast."

"You need a bath," Rosie said, looking her over. "You're filthy and you smell."

Sara laughed. "Thanks a lot."

Rosie grinned. "Here's the key to my house." She pulled her car keys out of her pocket and removed one from the key chain, handing it to Sara. "When I get home we can go over to the Pig and Pint."

"What about Kaliska?"

"We'll bring her along. I have a red wig you can wear if you're worried about being recognized."

"Does Raleigh go there?"

"It's a little low-brow for him, and besides, I think he's away at the moment. John will know."

"So Raleigh and John are buds now?"

"I wouldn't say that. You know John—he'll talk to anybody."

❧❧

When Sara entered the Pig and Pint she was wearing the red wig from when Rosie dressed up as Lucy from the I Love Lucy show, and sunglasses too big for her face. Her skin was tinged dark from Rosie's make-up and she had on a belted dress with red and white checks—the rest of the Lucy costume. It was too big and the worn cowboy boots that completed the outfit were too tight, which made her limp. Rosie led the way to a darkened corner and sat down. "I'll do the ordering," she whispered. "The only person here who might recognize you is John. Luckily he's too busy flirting with his new girlfriend."

Sara pulled over a highchair and slid the baby in, hoping she wouldn't decide to shift. She glanced toward the bar where her now overweight former boyfriend was leaning in to converse with a petite blonde. Definitely his type, Sara thought to herself. She chuckled, realizing that she'd been his type too, with her short blonde hair and small build. But in reality they'd had little in common.

Her thoughts roamed into the high hills to the cave, wondering if Istaga had returned and when he might arrive in Black Base to fetch her home. They'd had many arguments but he'd never taken off and stayed away like this.

"What can I get you, Rosie?" The young waiter stole a look at Sara and the baby, who was playing with several packets of sugar, and then turned back, waiting for Rosie's reply. Sara remembered that his name was Ed. He'd seen her many times in the past but he obviously had no idea who she was.

"Two Dos Equis, Ed. And a couple of hamburgers and maybe some chips?"

Once the beers came Rosie settled in, leaning on her elbows to talk with Sara. "The sound is off but watch the TV up there. The news is on."

Sara turned to look at the screen, startled to see a wild-eyed woman with short blonde hair sticking out from her head in tufts. The mud-streaked denim shirt exposed way too much of her thighs and her mouth was wide open as she screamed at Istaga/Coyote while pulling on his tail. Raleigh had already dropped to the ground and the viciousness of the attack made her gasp. "That's horrible," she whispered. "It didn't look so bad when I watched it before."

"Keep watching," Rosie said.

In the next shot Sara was running, holding a small limp form in her arms. A coyote followed her toward the weeds and a second later he was limping after her on two legs. "Wow. That didn't look real."

"That's what I was telling you. Everyone's saying that it's special effects. And with the way that guy recorded it with the cell phone moving all over the place it really seems fake."

Sara stared at her friend. "And yet two months later they're still playing it?"

The scene cut to the newscaster but with the sound turned off Sara had no idea what was going on. A moment later Raleigh's face appeared on camera, his neck covered in bandages. From his wild gestures Sara had a pretty good idea what he was saying. "Is he still healing this much later?" she asked looking at Rosie.

"It was pretty severe, Sara. And he has an axe to grind. He's trying to keep the story alive."

"Maybe they'll start to think he's some crazy guy on drugs," she whispered. "I should probably start a twitter feed to discredit him."

Rosie chuckled. "Maybe you should. From all the stuff he's tried to weasel out of, I think his reputation is a tad shabby."

Raleigh had been having an affair with Sara's mother at the same time he'd convinced Sara to take him back. He'd also murdered his best friend in order to cover up his criminal activities and then framed Sara for it. Apparently the police had failed to prove anything and so the man went free—pay-offs, she was sure. "I don't want to think about that time, Rosie. It was truly creepy."

"You don't have to, baby girl. You just have to take care of your family. I can discredit the man as well as anyone else. My twitter handle will be @truthbetold."

Sara chuckled. When the food came Sara let the baby gum a piece of bread while she and Rosie ate.

"How long are you staying?" Rosie asked.

"I haven't thought about it much. I can't go back up there, but what do I do about Istaga? He refuses to live in town. I expect him to come looking for us in a day or two and then I'll have to make a decision."

"It doesn't sound like an easy one," Rosie answered, gazing at the baby.

6

*C*oyote loped along the upper ridge feeling something that coyotes didn't feel. His body was heavy and hollow at the same time. When he spied Raven he stopped beneath the tree and looked up.

"What's wrong now, Coyote? You look like you lost your best friend."

"I did," he answered in coyote fashion.

"The woman is gone? What about your offspring?"

"Both gone."

"What foolish thing brought this about?"

"She wishes to live with humans and I do not."

"And yet you badgered the shaman to make you human. I told you nothing good would come of this."

"I should have listened to you but there was something driving me that I couldn't ignore."

"It's called love, you idiot. Now you've let it go. I feel sorry for you."

"What should I do?"

"How should I know? I'm just a bird."

"Please, Raven. You've advised me before."

Raven shook out his glossy black feathers and scraped his bill across the branch a couple of times before answering. Finally he cocked his head and focused one beady dark eye on Coyote. "If you want to be with the woman you have to give up this pride of yours."

"I don't know what that means."

"It means holding on to your ideas and not listening to hers. No relationship can withstand that kind of arrogance."

"So I should live in the human world and give up my true nature?"

"I didn't say that." Raven fixed him with his dark eye and then lifted into the air, loosening several dark feathers that landed on the ground at Coyote's feet. "Do what's in your heart," he cawed before the breeze took him.

Coyote mulled over Raven's words, trying very hard to think. Nearly every night he'd shifted unconsciously into Istaga and reached for Sara, always surprised and dismayed when she wasn't there. His dreams were filled with his past and how they'd met and what he felt for her—his obsession with becoming human so he could be with her. He remembered those first days when she'd taken him into her house and treated his wounds after she'd accidentally shot him. If it hadn't been for her and Raven's warnings he would have died. And then he thought of Kaliska and his heart would expand in his chest until he thought it would burst. Kaliska was his pup and Sara was his mate and coyotes mated for life.

7

"Not sure this was the best idea you've ever had," Rosie said, looking Sara over. "You look like a person who's been on the lam and might be a little more than slightly deranged."

Sara ran her fingers through her hair, feeling the short tufts that indicated a very bad haircut. It was her own fault for not using a mirror. "Someone can fix it, can't they?"

Rosie cocked her head to one side, studying her. "It has to grow in order to be fixed. But that isn't the worst of it. Now that you've been here for a while I've had a chance to see how thin you are. Your cheeks are hollow and there's a wild look in your eyes that wasn't there before. Your mental state is not good, Sara."

"I expected Istaga to come and find us by now. Where is he? I can't stay with you forever and I need to know what I'm doing."

"That doesn't explain why you're not eating. The baby needs to be weaned. She's draining you."

I'm fine, Rosie," Sara said, glancing down at the baby at her breast.

"You indicated you want to get Kaliska into the pre-school here. You'll have to come up with a living situation that they accept as well as an appearance that doesn't scare the bejesus out of them. At this point you look more animal than human."

Sara buttoned her shirt and put Kaliska on the floor before heading to the mirror on the front wall. A wild-eyed woman with dark circles under her eyes stared back, uneven tufts of blonde hair sticking straight up. Her lips were chapped to the point of bleeding and her collarbones jutted out like bird wings. Rosie was right. Tears filled her eyes before she turned away. "We were up there for several months, Rosie. I guess I wasn't eating enough. There were no mirrors. Things just went too far."

Rosie shook her head and went into the kitchen. "You're here now and you need to eat. I'm fixing us a good Mexican dinner tonight full of lots of fat. You need to put on some weight and get some color in those pale cheeks of yours before you go out in public again."

In bed in the spare room that night Sara's thoughts turned to Istaga. She'd been here over a week and he hadn't come looking for her. Was this the end for them? She turned to gaze down at the baby girl asleep next to her. She smoothed the blonde hair back from her round face, a wave of love moving through her. Kaliska asked for her Da every day, making Sara feel terrible about ripping her away from her father. Kaliska seemed to shift into coyote whenever she thought about him and that would definitely cause a problem in a school situation. It was great being with Rosie and she liked using Rosie's computer while she was at work, but it wasn't enough without Istaga in her life. She and

Kaliska both needed him.

֍֍

Rosie was in the kitchen the next morning when Sara came in for coffee with the baby on her hip. As she poured her first cup Rosie showed her the paper.

"This story refuses to go away. People are still wondering what happened that night. Your ex--or are you still married--has launched another campaign to find you. He's been on the news again and seems determined to prove that you're a freak and need to be locked up. He's going on again about the crime you supposedly committed three years ago, adding that to your latest list of offenses. He sure knows how to get the press on his side."

Sara read the article on page four; she was glad it wasn't headline news. Shape-shifters will be found, it said at the top, continuing with a statement from Raleigh vowing to find his wife and her beast lover and put them in jail for attempted murder and bestiality. A grainy picture of her and Istaga had been added. Sara handed the paper back, too upset to read further. Maybe coming back hadn't been such a good idea after all. But then again the idea of being stuck up in those mountains was even worse. "I have to change my appearance."

"That's what I'm workin' on," Rosie said, placing a plate heaped with eggs, tortillas and beans in front of her. "Eat up."

"I'm not very hungry."

Rosie gave her a look that caused her to pick up her

fork. After one bite she put the fork down. "I'm talking about more than weight here. I need to dye my hair or buy a wig or get a face-lift or something."

"A face-lift?" Rosie made a derisive sound in the back of her throat.

Sara smiled wanly and pulled the baby into her lap. "Can she eat beans?"

"Why not? She's old enough for regular food."

With Kaliska helping Sara managed to get through about half of the breakfast Rosie had prepared.

"I'm off," Rosie announced a short time later. "If you need to leave her with me for an hour or so I get a lunch break at noon."

Sara smiled. "Thanks for everything, Rosie. I'm glad you're my friend."

Rosie made a face and shook her head. "A stray dog is what you are. And I always was a sucker for them. See you later."

8

Istaga headed down the mountain, the rifle he'd stolen from Raleigh's truck slung over his shoulder, stolen bullets in his jeans pocket. He followed an animal path that most humans would not be able to see, his nose attuned to dung and urine. If he had known how he would feel without Sara and Kaliska he never would have stayed away those two nights. A full turning of the moon and more had gone by since then and his moods had grown darker and darker. Raven's words hung around him like a taunt: "Do what's in your heart." Sara and his baby were the two most important things in his life. As far as doing what was in his heart, he wasn't sure what those words meant. His heart was there to pump blood into his veins when he was hunting—to give him the stamina to catch the rabbits and other small animals he ate.

Another word that mystified him was the one Sara used when referring to how she felt about him. 'Love' joined 'heart' in a category of untranslatable concepts. What he felt for Sara and Kaliska could not be explained by one word—when he saw the two of them his tail lifted, and he had an urge to let out a howl of pure joy and sometimes did. If he was human at the time his chest felt full, and his body felt light, like maybe he could fly.

He'd been walking for a while when something in the bushes made him stop and listen. A twig had snapped in the trees to his left. Whatever it was, it was big. A second later a heavy man burst out of the trees, his eyes widening when he saw Istaga. "I didn't know there were any injuns' up here."

Istaga didn't reply, just took his measure, his nose picking up the nervous sweat and the tinge of beer on the man's breath. Something told him not to engage.

"Are you deaf and dumb?"

Istaga turned his back and continued down the trail.

"Hey! I was talkin' to you!" When a hand came on his shoulder, Istaga whirled, pulling the rifle off his other shoulder at the same time.

"Hey, hey," the man said, lifting up his hands. "Just tryin' to be friendly. There aren't many people to talk to around these parts. Are you with the predator masters? You Injuns are pretty good hunters but don't you usually use a bow and arrows?" The man laughed at his own joke and then spat brown liquid out of the side of his mouth. "I got separated from the others. We left a couple of coyotes over that way if you have a mind to skin them." He pointed into the trees in the direction he'd come from. "I'll give you ten percent of what we get for 'em."

Istaga snarled under his breath, trying hard not to shift and kill this man.

"We were supposed to leave a month ago but a couple of us decided to keep at it for a while. It's so damn easy to pick them off—like taking candy from a baby."

He pulled something out of his pocket and blew into it, producing a sound that Istaga recognized as a young coyote in distress. Istaga grabbed it out of the man's hand and broke it into several pieces.

"What'd you do that for? Those things are expensive."

"I suggest you and your friends get out of here," Istaga said, cocking his rifle. "If you don't I can't be responsible for what might happen."

"Are you threatening me?"

Before the man could remove his own rifle from his shoulder Istaga had grabbed it away from him. "Yes, I am."

"I'm going to report you," the man said, backing away. "You can't just take a man's property like that."

"Have you noticed the no hunting signs up here? This is protected wilderness."

The man laughed, spitting again. "No one knows we're here and you're not the law. I have friends in high places in the Fish and Game Department. They'll get me off if it comes to that."

The urge to shift was almost too much for Istaga, his eyes narrowing as he fought his instinct. He could easily kill this man for what he and his friends had done, a vision of the coyote carcasses making his stomach churn.

The man reached forward. "Now give me my gun back and maybe I'll skedaddle like you asked."

Someone called out a name and the man turned, cupping his hands to call back. "I'm over here, Bob!"

A few moments later another man joined them, a pistol held in his right hand and pointed straight at Istaga. "Who the hell are you?"

Istaga sniffed, picking up the scent of blood. The man wore a knife on his belt, a bloody coyote pelt slung over his shoulder with the head still intact. His stomach contracted in pain.

"You don't look too scary to me with your buckshot rifle. This gun will put a hole in you the size of a golf ball."

Istaga didn't ask what a golf ball was as rage filled his entire body. Before he could stop himself he was on all fours, his mouth open as he lunged at the man with the pistol. He leapt pushing him backward, the pelt falling with him. The gun went off, a bullet grazing his shoulder and taking fur with it. He ignored the pain as his teeth sank deep into the flesh of the man's upper arm, tearing through muscle and tendon and leaving a wide bleeding gash. By this time the other man was screaming at the top of his lungs, the hysterical sound grating in Coyote's sensitive ears.

He was moving toward the fragile skin of the throat when something in the back of his mind told him to stop—he fought against the voice, but in the end he pulled away. The injured man was shrieking now and holding his hand against his arm to stem the blood that gushed between his fingers. If other hunters were in this forest they would surely hear him.

Coyote shifted, grabbed the two rifles and the pistol and took off down the hill as though the fires of hell were after him. Behind him the yelling continued, growing fainter as he wound his way through the forest, following a trail that only he could discern.

⟡⟡⟡

Istaga stopped late in the night, his muscles giving way with exhaustion. He felt water on his face and knew he was doing what Sara did sometimes— something she called crying. His chest felt tight as the water kept coming and then a sound came up from his throat and lifted into the silence, scaring him with its intensity. His arm burned where the blood had coagulated and dried. He let out a human cry of pure agony and then shifted, too tired to worry about his wound or hunters finding him; he couldn't stand the sensations moving through this human body another second. With the guns lying next to him he curled up under thick bushes and went to sleep.

It was daybreak when he woke in human form and picked up the guns. He headed along the edge of a rocky hillside before descending onto the paved road below. When he reached a small town he found the nearest bar, his only thought to drink the fiery liquid that soothed him.

"Where'd you come from?" the barkeep asked, his wary gaze on the rifles slung over Istaga's shoulder. "Are you one of those coyote hunters?"

Istaga fought the bile that crept up his throat. "No. But I ran into a couple of them up there." He pointed vaguely toward the mountain. "They were hunting illegally so I took their weapons away."

The man seemed to pale a little before asking what

he wanted to drink.

"I don't have any money," Istaga said, "but I could trade one of these rifles for a good meal and a few beers."

The man brightened as he stared at the Remington with the sight on top. "Are you serious? Hell yes, and I'll throw in a good bottle of whiskey to boot."

Istaga found a table and sank down before pulling back his shirt to take a look at the wound on his shoulder. It seemed to have closed up but it still hurt like hell. If Sara were here she'd know what to do. A pang went through his mid-section as her face appeared in his mind.

He looked up when a young woman came over and pulled out the chair next to him. "Harry said you might like a little company," she said, slipping into the seat. "You look like you were rode hard and put up wet."

Istaga stared at her, unable to comprehend what she was saying.

"Harry says he'll throw my services into your deal."

"Services?" Istaga had a vague recollection of another encounter with a woman he'd had in the past. But that one hadn't mentioned 'services' only that she was available. But this one was younger with dark eyes and sharp features and seemed nervous.

"I'm Estelle," she said, holding out her hand.

"Istaga."

"You look awful tired, Istaga. I have a little place across the street. After your meal we could go over there and you could take a rest."

Istaga was exhausted and the idea of sleeping in a bed sounded very good to him.

"So, you two make a deal?" the barkeep asked, plunking down a plate filled with meat and eggs and several other things that Istaga couldn't identify.

Estelle smiled. "He's coming over to my place after breakfast."

It was less than an hour later that Istaga picked up the bottle of amber liquid and followed Estelle across the street and into a ramshackle hut. His nose was assaulted by the varying smells of perfume, cooked food and a scent that reminded him of the little boxes where humans let their water go.

"Bed's in there," Estelle said, pointing toward a beaded curtain.

Istaga went through and lay down on the lumpy mattress letting out a long sigh. He was almost asleep when Estelle came in.

"Why don't you take off that shirt and jeans?" she asked. "I can rub your back and put some salve on that cut on your arm."

Istaga thought of Sara's herbal cures, hoping Estelle could get rid of the burning sensation that refused to go away. He sat up and pulled off his jeans and unbuttoned his shirt before taking a long swig of the burning liquid.

"Oh, honey, that looks nasty," Estelle said, peering down at his arm.

She went to a rickety piece of furniture and pulled open a drawer. "This antibacterial salve should help," she muttered. Before returning she stepped out of her long skirt and then pulled her blouse over her head.

Istaga was drinking from the bottle and didn't pay much attention as she came back and climbed on the bed next to him. "This should make it feel better," she said, slathering the gooey gel into his wound. It did seem to cool it down. He placed the bottle on the table and lay back and closed his eyes, but when her hands began roaming across his body they flew open.

"You have a nice body," she said.

Istaga couldn't think, all his senses concentrated on where her fingers were. When she lay down next to him he pressed against her. He felt the softness of her, the rounded edges where Sara's body jutted, smelled the sweat that had beaded between her large breasts and on her upper lip. She wasn't Sara but it didn't matter. Nothing mattered but the urgency of what he was feeling.

"Why are you here?"

Coyote looked around, trying to track down the source of the voice. It seemed vaguely familiar. He finally spied Raven in the branches of the tree next to him. But he didn't remember falling asleep here, he thought, looking around at the tall trees and the wide slash of blue above.

"Where is here?" he asked.

"It's the realm of the raven, Coyote. "You are far from the human world. You won't escape without sprouting wings."

Wings? Coyote stood up to look around surprised to see

a misty valley in the far distance. They were on a ridge that seemed impossibly high and very narrow where nothing was familiar. "How did I get here?"

Raven clacked his beak together and then made a sound that resembled a laugh. "How would I know?"

"I have no memory of it," Coyote mumbled.

"Maybe you've stumbled onto the spirit trail again," Raven continued, peering down with one bright eye.

Coyote didn't respond, thinking that Raven might be right. But what was he here to learn this time?

Raven cawed and then rose into the air and when Coyote looked up there were a million ravens in the sky swooping and lifting on the thermals as they made intricate dancing patterns above him. "Wait!" he called, but the bird was already gone. When he turned a Native man dressed in deerskin shirt and pants was standing close, his impassive gaze trained on Coyote's face.

"Istaga, you must listen closely," the man said.

"Toh Yah? Is that you?" he asked, wondering if this was the same man who had helped him out three years before. He owed Toh Yah his life many times over.

But the man only watched him without expression, finally saying, "You have lost your way and that is why you've come here. Your pride has separated you from those you love and to reach them you must give up this part of yourself. What will you leave behind to signify your sincerity?"

Coyote looked down to see that he'd shifted into human form without knowing it. He searched through his jeans pockets and the one in his plaid shirt, coming up empty-handed. "I have nothing to leave behind."

The man came close and reached up to touch the turquoise beads Istaga always wore around his neck. "What about this?"

"You gave me those for protection," Istaga said.

"This is another time, Istaga, another place." He held out his hand, waiting until Istaga reached around to unclasp the beads. Once Istaga had placed them in his hand he turned to leave.

"But what am I to learn?" Istaga cried, feeling suddenly naked and lost without his talisman.

"You'll know when it happens," the man answered. He seemed to fade like smoke and then he was gone.

Istaga woke with an intake of breath and sat up. He was still in Estelle's bed but she was gone. The first thing he did was reach for his beads, but sure enough his necklace was no longer around his neck. Did Estelle take them? Surely those stones were valuable in the human world. Dream or no dream, something had happened. And it left him with a very uneasy feeling.

He knew without having to think about it that Sara would be very upset by what he and Estelle had done together. But how could he resist? It was a natural act between male and female. Was this what Toh Yah meant by 'he'd lost his way' and if so how was he to find it again?

He stumbled to his feet, noticing the empty bottle on the table. Had he really consumed the entire bottle of what Toh Yah called 'firewater'? His head spun as he searched for his clothes, the urge to howl rising into his throat along with a sharp feeling that made him want to bring up the contents of his stomach. Half-dressed he lurched outside and retched into the weeds and then moved behind the small shack to let his water go.

Inside again he pulled on his jeans, gathered his one remaining rifle and pistol and left the house, moving into the empty field next to the road.

9

"The red hair looks good on you," Rosie said, admiring Sara's hennaed short curls.

Sara ran her fingers through it, making it stand up. "Had to do something to keep from being recognized."

"Getting a job in San Manuel was a smart move. Not many people from Black Base go that far north for a restaurant."

Sara had recently acquired a waitressing job in a town twenty-five miles north and was getting ready to head out. "I hope you're right. It seems like someone's working hard to keep this damn story alive."

"I think your decision about Kaliska was wise." Rosie glanced over at the wire cage where Kaliska, in coyote form, gnawed on a bone. "You can't take a chance with her right now."

"It worries me to leave her alone, though," Sara answered watching her two-year-old. "She's used to nursing at least once during the day—sometimes twice." Sara looked down at her chest. "And I'm used to it too."

Rosie scoffed. "She's old enough to give up mother's milk, Sara. It's time you weaned her."

Sara frowned. She liked nursing her baby and the closeness that came from it. She hadn't planned on weaning her for another six months. "At least I'll be here to feed her in the evening."

Rosie pressed her full lips together and shook her head in disapproval. "She can't get into anything from in there and I'll be back around noon to check on her."

The pre-school idea had been scrapped after it became apparent that the child was too young to control her impulses. The day Rosie hauled the enormous cage home in the back of her truck Sara had been skeptical, and after three hours of howling from Kaliska she'd nearly given up. But now it seemed Kaliska had grown used to it, spending most of her day in coyote form to chew on the rubber squeaky toys or meat bones they left her with. A bowl of water and one of kibble sat in one corner. The only problem so far had been her inability to hold her pee and poop for any length of time. And in human form she was far from potty trained.

"Okay, I'm off," Sara said, opening the door. "Are you sure it's okay if I use the truck?"

Rosie nodded. "I can walk and I don't have anything to do today that requires wheels."

"I've got to find a beater," Sara muttered. "I'll see you this afternoon and don't forget to lock the door when you leave."

The truck roared to life as soon as Sara turned the key and she rumbled down the road toward the small café in San Manuel.

As the desert landscape flew by Sara revisited her bewilderment about Istaga. Why hadn't he shown up? It had been nearly three months now. She couldn't live with Rosie forever but getting a place for only herself and Kaliska didn't feel right somehow. She loved and missed her mate but these past months had made it clear that she could no longer live out in the boonies eating raw meat and doing nothing but hunting, mating and sleeping.

If she weaned Kaliska there was a good chance she would get pregnant--she couldn't risk having another baby who might or might not be all coyote or half coyote. The only other solution was stocking up on birth control pills, but if she were a coyote when they mated that wouldn't do much good. She shook her head, wondering why her thoughts had drifted into this subject. Istaga wasn't here so why was she worrying about pregnancy? Maybe there was a part of her that *did* want another baby—or maybe it was just the sex she missed. Her former feelings of dissatisfaction had faded, leaving only the hollowness of Istaga's absence.

Thank goodness she had a job--money in her pocket. Even if it wasn't that exciting she felt productive and enjoyed the conversations she had with customers. Once she'd saved enough money she planned to buy a used computer and get her web design business going again. She'd even talked to Joe, the owner of the café, about setting up a site for him.

Of course she would have to start from scratch with her new name that now felt like her own. Sunny Sullivan was the perfect alias, simple and easy to remember.

But her nights were not so down to earth and practical, her thoughts about Istaga keeping her awake for many hours. And then the fears would begin—was he dead? Didn't he care about her and Kaliska? Had he found a new mate and taken off into the mountains of Mexico? It was entirely possible that she would never see him again. And then she would cry as silently as she could, trying not to wake the sleeping baby next to her.

↬↬

Joe was just unlocking the front door when Sara pulled into the gravel driveway. She drove the truck around back and slid into the spot next to his jeep and cut the engine. The screen door squeaked when she opened it and headed into the back room where they stored extra food. She went from there into the kitchen, returning Joe's smile of welcome.

"Glad you're here, Sunny. There's a big party coming in early. They belong to that hunting group—you know the ones."

Sara blanched. "The predator hunters?"

"Yeah, that's the one. They'll need a hearty breakfast before they head out."

And maybe a little rat poison in their coffee, Sara thought to herself.

It was a half hour later that a group of five beefy men arrived through the front door, their faces pink with excitement.

"And you wouldn't believe the size of the f-ing coyote he turned into," one of them said, causing Sara to prick up her ears. "He almost killed Bob."

"So he just attacked for no reason? Why the hell

didn't you shoot the son-of-a-bitch?"

"He shifted and took off with all our guns." There was a titter of laughter from one or two, as if they didn't believe it.

Sara brought over a pot of coffee and filled their cups, hoping to hear more, but they had changed the topic to where they could find the biggest group of coyotes to slaughter.

She brought them their plates of ham and bacon and eggs, their pancakes slathered in butter, hoping that at least one or two would die of a heart attack while they were out hunting.

Just before they left—without leaving her a tip— they brought it up again.

"I told Fish and Game," one of them said, "and I spoke to a reporter because of what happened a couple months back. Someone should catch that creep and put him out of his misery. He's a freak of nature."

"Did they believe you?" one of the men asked, looking skeptical.

"I don't know. We didn't have cell reception or I would have caught it on my phone. But I'll tell you one thing—I'd know that dude anywhere and if I ever see him again, I'll..." his voice faded as they walked out the door, but Sara had a pretty good idea what the end of the sentence was.

"What's wrong with you?" Joe's voice sounded annoyed and worried at the same time as he watched her staring after them.

"I hate those predator hunters," she answered, trying to act normal as she picked up the greasy plates.

"They do us all a service, Sunny. Coyotes prey on the livestock."

"That's hogwash! Coyotes eat rabbits and small game—they never go after cows or even calves. They'd have to be starving to do that."

Joe stared at her. "You seem pretty worked up like you have some personal interest in this."

"I do, Joe. I happen to believe that wild animals have as much a right to be here as we do, maybe even more so. And those guys don't give a crap about anything but acting like a bunch of trigger happy a-holes." Sara stormed into the kitchen, threw the dirty dishes into the sink and then flung open the screen door, letting it bang as she went outside.

"Sunny, we have other customers coming in!" Joe yelled.

But Sara was beyond hearing him as she put the truck into reverse, spinning gravel as she backed up. Black smoke spewed out of the tailpipe as she roared away.

Halfway to Black Base she pulled off the highway and gave herself over to tears. She wailed and screamed at the thought of Istaga on the mountain fighting off predator hunters. Where was he? And worse than that, was he all right?

༒

Rosie took hold of Sara's shoulders. "Calm down, Sara! Start at the beginning and please try to make sense this time."

"I know why the story won't die, Rosie," Sara said,

rubbing at her tear-streaked face. "Istaga shifted in front of some hunters up in the mountains—from what they said he tried to kill one of them. I'm sure they've told local reporters all about it."

"I haven't heard anything about this."

"Why would you? You hardly watch TV except when we go to the Pig and Pint."

Sara checked where they stood outside Rosie's place of work, making sure no one was in hearing distance. Luckily no one was on a smoking break and no cars were parked close.

Rosie took hold of her arm. "Have you been home yet?"

"No, I came straight here. I had to talk to someone who would understand. Actually the only person who would," Sara added, staring at her friend.

"Go home and wash your face and spend time with your baby. I'll try to take off early."

❧

Kaliska had made a mess of the cage and it took Sara a while to clean it. She put the pup in the bathtub and while she was soaping her fur she shifted, letting out a happy chortle as she splashed in the water. For a moment Sara was taken out of her worries, sharing her baby's joy. After the bath Sara wrapped her in a towel and then went into the bedroom to nurse her.

"Whew! It stinks in here. Where are you?"

"In here!" Sara called. No matter what was going on, the simple act of feeding her child managed to assuage something deep inside her. She couldn't stand the idea of giving it up.

Rosie poked her head around the partially closed bedroom door. "When you get done with that I have some news."

Sara's heart did a little flip-flop, her moment of happiness gone in a flash. "Did you see the news?"

"I'll tell you all about it when you get out here."

By now the baby had begun to fidget, losing interest in milk as she craned her neck to see Rosie. Sara put a cloth diaper on her before allowing her to toddle into the other room. By the time she'd cleaned up the bathroom and hung up the towels Kaliska was in Rosie's lap playing with the silver and turquoise necklace around Rosie's neck.

Sara flopped into the one overstuffed chair. "Well?"

"I went by the Pig and Pint and guess who was there?"

"The hunters?"

Rosie nodded, a frown marring her normally smooth forehead. "They were bragging about how many animals they killed today."

"Did they mention...?"

"I was getting to that. I think the story's been embellished since this morning, but they mentioned some wild crazed animal the size of Godzilla that attacked them and would have killed the one called Bob if his buddy hadn't dragged the animal off. According to their story the oversized coyote turned into an enormous Indian who took off into the forest. It sounded like they were describing Bigfoot."

"What was the reaction?"

"Some people were wide-eyed, others just turned away. According to them it should be on the news in the next day or two."

"If they were the same guys from this morning the story was second-hand. Was this Bob guy there?"

"Oh yeah. And his arm had the bandage to prove his injury."

Sara stared out the window noticing smoke in the far distance. "There's a fire somewhere in the mountains," she said, standing to get a better look.

Rosie turned, shifting the baby onto her other knee. "Looks like a big one."

"Those mountains are where Istaga and I were living. I hope he isn't still there."

"It's also where those hunters said this incident happened. I wonder if they started it." She shook her head. "It's always these idiots from out of town who burn down our forests. I wish there was a law against them."

10

$\mathcal{C}$oyote climbed the hill, his lungs burning. The pine forest where he and Sara had lived was on fire. He fought the urge to howl, knowing instinctively that this would only make matters worse. Flames licked at the tops of the trees lower in the valley, wind throwing sparks from branch to branch as the fire worked its way upward. He could hear the whoosh as dry branches caught, catching sight of the plume of gray that lifted into a sky already dark. After scanning in every direction and lifting his nose to detect the wind currents he headed west and down.

He'd been traveling for days trying to warn other coyotes about the hunters, but so far had had little success. They did not respond to his warning calls, as though they knew he was the one who had defected from their ranks three years before; news in the coyote world spread even faster than in the human one. He was exhausted, frustrated, and lonely for his family, but he also felt a burning obligation to take care of his own.

Because of the need to think like a human he shifted into Istaga. He wondered if he should head toward Page to find his friend Toh Yah. The man had helped Istaga and Sara escape the authorities before the birth of their cub. Istaga had a feeling he was also responsible for Sara's sudden ability to shift. If it hadn't been for Toh Yah both of them would be in jail. But with Raleigh's recent appearance the same problems were coming up again. The man was determined to ruin Sara's life only because she'd rejected him.

It was hard for Istaga to understand the ways of humans—the need to possess, not to mention living a life of lies. But then he thought of Toh Yah. Native Americans did not view the world this way. They cherished the earth and were a part of it, not like the white men who seemed to think it was their right to take everything the earth had to offer with little regard for the consequences.

He went fast, skirting around trees and trying to hold his breath. The dry tinder crackled and spit as it caught, causing sweat to pour off him. If he didn't reach the valley before this section burned he would burn with it.

By the time he reached the valley and came out of the path of the fire he'd changed his mind about traveling to Page. It was very far from this mountain range and the thought of being even further away from Sara and Kaliska made him reconsider. Before he could think it through he was Coyote and Coyote knew exactly what he had to do.

.

It was dry summer now and Coyote's pads were cut and bleeding from running hard. He'd spent most days hiding under mesquite bushes or in dry ravines waiting until the cool of night to travel. Game was hard to come by and water nearly nonexistent. Raven had visited him several times but he wasn't sure if the bird had been a hallucination or real. Whatever Raven had told him had disappeared from his mind. He came to a stop on the outskirts of Black Base and shifted for the first time in days. His human body felt alien and he didn't like the sick feeling in the pit of his stomach. Had he eaten something bad? Or was this what Sara called an 'emotion' he needed to look at— another 'feeling' that pertained to what he was doing? He couldn't decipher it—he didn't have the tools and at this moment he wondered why he'd ever wanted to become human in the first place. If it wasn't for Sara and Kaliska he would have found a coyote pack and been long gone by now.

11

$\int$ara returned to the Desert Café the next morning and apologized to Joe. Luckily he was desperate for her help and forgave her for running out on him during the busy morning shift.

"But please, Sunny, no more politics interfering with your work. Can you promise me that?"

Sara gazed into his kind face feeling a sharp pang of guilt. It wasn't his fault the hunters ate here. He couldn't exactly choose his customers. "I promise," she said, tying the apron around her waist.

The day went by quickly with a steady flow of customers and when the shift ended at three Sara counted up her tips. Forty dollars was a good haul considering the clientele that frequented these parts. It wasn't exactly downtown Tucson, was it?

"Have a good fourth!" she called as she walked out the back door. How it had become July was a mystery. She and Istaga had been apart for over four months.

As she drove back to Rosie's in Rosie's truck her mind went to her situation. It was past time to find a car and a place of her own. As always this led into thoughts of Istaga, the usual pain radiating around her heart. Where was he? Maybe over the four-day weekend she would take a little trip up into the mountains to find him.

❧

When Sara walked through the door Rosie was waiting for her. "I have a hankering for a beer and a bowl of chips and guacamole. How about it?"

Sara was tired but the look on Rosie's face told her that she needed to agree. Besides, it would be the perfect time to ask her if she'd mind taking care of Kaliska over the weekend. "Do I have time to nurse her?"

Rosie shrugged, turning away. Sara knew how Rosie felt about weaning Kaliska but without Istaga in her life it was one of the few things she looked forward to. Her life seemed to have come down to going to work and coming home, her nights filled with bad dreams. Kaliska was the one thing that brought her joy.

Kaliska was on the floor playing with a soft stuffed animal that Rosie had gotten her but as soon as she saw her mother she stood and toddled toward her. "Hello, sweetie," Sara said, lifting her and cradling her against her chest. She sat on the couch and unbuttoned her shirt, arranging the baby on her lap. "What should we do with Kaliska while we're gone?" she asked.

"Just lock her in the cage. We won't be gone long. She seems to enjoy her time in there."

Sara tried not to feel skeptical about this pronouncement. "Is that true, Kaliska?" she asked, gazing down on her soft blonde curls. "Do you want to go in your cage?"

Kaliska let go of the breast, her blue eyes wide as they met Sara's. She wriggled off her mother's lap and toddled toward the cage.

"She wants her bone," Rosie said, heading into the kitchen. When Rosie came back she was holding a meat bone. Kaliska shifted into a coyote and wagged her tail. "See?" Rosie opened the cage door and threw the bone inside. A second later the coyote pup was inside the cage and had settled in for a good chew.

Sara stared in disbelief. A bone was better than nursing? When her gaze met Rosie's it was obvious by Rosie's expression that she understood what Sara was thinking.

"If you don't wean her she'll wean herself," Rosie said.

Sara didn't respond to that pronouncement as she gazed at the coyote in the cage. The pup was getting big now, almost too big for the size of the enclosure.

Sara didn't bother to change for the trip to the Pig and Pint. Everyone wore jeans, most ripped and dirty. At least hers were clean and she'd thought to wear a clean shirt to work this morning. She re-buttoned her shirt and tucked it in and then took a look in the mirror. Her cheeks were not as hollow as they had been four months ago, but her eyes were still hollow and sad. What was she thinking the day she left the mountains? Her thoughts of being in human company for a few days had turned into months now—months in which she'd grown more and more lonely for her mate. A vision of Coyote shot and bleeding to death appeared in her mind, making her heart race. If she didn't find him this weekend she wasn't sure what she would do.

Rosie went to the bar to grab a couple of beers while Sara found a table in the back. Despite her new hair color she was still worried about being recognized. The shifting story wasn't front and center anymore but it appeared on the news from time to time. And because of Raleigh she was wanted by the police--it wouldn't do to have someone put two and two together. That's why she was surprised when John walked over and sat down.

"Hey, Sara," he said before taking a swig from the beer bottle he'd carried with him. He grinned at her and then wiped his mouth with the back of his hand.

"Shh," Rosie hissed, putting her hand on his arm as she arrived at the table. She put the bottles on the table and sat next to Sara.

John looked surprised. "Did you think I wouldn't recognize you? We spent several months together, Sara. Just because you dye your hair another color doesn't mean I wouldn't know you." He chuckled, staring at her. "You have a distinctive way of walking and cocking your head to one side."

"So you just ignored me all those other times I was in here?" Sara whispered.

"I saw you but I knew you were trying to go incognito. I have to say you look better than you did a couple of months ago." He sat back and looked her over in an appraising way before continuing. "What brought you back here, anyway? That Raleigh guy is still in the news. I'm surprised he hasn't managed to throw you in jail."

"Is he? We don't have a TV."

"You're not missing much," John said, tipping his chair back. "I won't give you away but I'd be careful. Raleigh seems to be a real a-hole."

"Hellooo," Sara said, drawing the word out. "I told you that a couple of years ago. Why do you think I moved here in the first place?"

"Where's that guy you were so hot and bothered about? I saw him back in the winter but he hasn't shown up lately."

Sara's stomach tilted. "I don't know where he is."

"Last time he was in here he was asking me all about the predator masters, you know, that..."

"I know all about it, John. And I'd rather not think about them."

"Did you know Raleigh's part of their group?"

Sara was beginning to feel sick. "I do know that. Can we drop it?"

"Sure thing, babe."

"And don't call me babe. Where's that new chickie you were with the last time I was here?"

John grinned. "So you *do* still care. Cherry moved back to Cincinnati. I'm available, if that's why you're asking."

Sara stared at him in disgust. His beer belly had grown several inches and his manner had become even more obnoxious. "It isn't," she answered.

"I know something that'll interest you, if you haven't already heard. Raleigh comes to Black Base all the time now. He bought a cabin up in the mountains."

"You don't need to tell her that," Rosie said, shooting him a hostile look. "She's had enough bad dealings with that man."

"I'm only warning her to watch out for him. That last fiasco was too much. I'm still wondering how that guy did it."

Sara frowned. "What are you talking about?"

"The shifting, Sara. You must have caught it on the news at the time. It showed you and that weirdo you were hanging out with shifting into coyotes. What kind of camera did that guy have? He's become a minor celebrity in certain occult circles. And did you hear about the hunters who insisted they saw some dude shift into a coyote? Apparently this coyote was a hell of a monster and nearly killed one of them." John let out a guffaw and then belched. "What a load of hooey. This place is turning into Area 51."

"Let's get out of here," Rosie said. She tipped her beer up slugging down what remained. "And you should keep this crap to yourself, John. Sara's been through enough."

Sara got to her feet and followed Rosie out of the bar. When she glanced back, John shrugged, his mouth turning up in a wry grin.

"What a jerk," Rosie said as they headed to the truck. "If I'd known he was there I never would have suggested it."

"At least now I know that Raleigh hasn't given up. And if he's spending a lot of time here I should move somewhere else."

"Do you think he's still looking for you?"

"After the shifting incident? Are you kidding? He would dearly love to see me behind bars and I shudder to think what he might like to do with Kaliska. If he got his hands on her she'd end up in a lab somewhere with needles and wires stuck in her. I wonder what possessed him to spend so much time here? I thought he just liked the fat cats he hung out with up in Duluth. I have a bad feeling it's related to me--he's intent on putting me away for good. Maybe something came up about Lee's death and he wants to make sure I'm the one who pays for his crime. "

Rosie parked the truck in the usual place and headed to the house, but at the steps she paused. "Didn't we lock the door?"

Sara took one look at the open door and sprinted into the house, her gaze going to the cage. The enclosure stood open and Kaliska was gone. "Raleigh has her!" she shrieked.

"Wait a second, Sara. He doesn't know me or that you're living here." Rosie took Sara by the arm and led her to the couch. "Sit." She perused the room. "Who would take her stuffed toy, her bone and her clothes?" she asked.

Sara jumped up. "It must have been Istaga, but why didn't he stay?"

"I don't know, but I feel better knowing she's with him."

Sara felt tears well. "He doesn't love me," she sobbed, flinging herself down on the couch. "All he cares about is Kaliska."

"Maybe something happened to scare him. You

know how wary he is."

"I'll go look. Maybe he's still around." Sara was up and out the door and barely heard Rosie's warning of 'be careful.'

Sara searched up and down the street and then decided it would be easier as a coyote. At least that way she could track him. She did what she normally did, making the decision to become coyote, but nothing happened. Trying a second time brought the same result. What was this now—some trick of fate to make her even more crazy?

She sat on the curb and put her head in her hands. This was all her fault. If she hadn't stayed away the three of them would be together. But what if it wasn't Istaga at all, what if someone else had broken in and taken her baby? She couldn't go to the police.

When Sara entered the house a few minutes later Rosie took one look at her before holding her arms out. Sara let herself be held, trying to control her sobs.

"I can't shift and if I can't shift I can't find them!" she wailed. "And what if it wasn't Istaga? What if some freak has her? Oh my god Rosie, what am I going to do?"

"We'll find her," Rosie answered, smoothing the hair back from Sara's forehead. "I'm sure she's with her father."

Sara pictured the two of them, the beer in her stomach turning to acid. If Istaga had her where would he go? Her plans for the weekend just became more important than ever.

12

The bad feeling was back in his stomach and this time Coyote had to heave up the contents of his stomach. The pup watched him with interest, her ears pricked forward. When she shifted to human Coyote decided to join her. Maybe the sickness would go away. But instead of going away it was worse, making him feel weak all over with an ache in his chest that he couldn't ignore. He knew these human bodies were fragile and wondered if he should seek help.

"Dada," Kaliska said, hugging him around the legs.

He bent down and picked her up and then pressed her little body against his. The ache was almost too much for him, but this one was different. Why did these bodies have to ache and hurt and make water come out of his eyes? What did this do for the species?

"Da cry," Kaliska said, reaching out to touch his face where tears were rolling down. "No sad," she said, scrunching up her forehead.

"I don't know if I'm sad or happy, Kaliska," he whispered. "When did you learn to talk?"

"Where Mommy?" Kaliska asked, looking around.

"Mommy's not here," Istaga answered, before breaking down completely. He sobbed uncontrollably and when he glanced at Kaliska her eyes were wide with fear. What in Raven's name was he doing? Why hadn't he waited for Sara to come home? Tracking Kaliska to that house had been easy but his hasty decision had now left him feeling confused and upset. But the idea of going back was even worse. Sara would be angry and hurt. It would make this body feel worse than it already did. Why had she left their baby alone and locked inside a cage? If he'd done something like that she'd be furious. He wiped his eyes with his sleeve. If Sara wanted to be with him she would have returned to the mountains a long time ago. Anger replaced his sadness. "Let's be coyotes, Kaliska. We can hunt and find a pack to travel with. We'll have fun."

Kaliska looked down at her stuffed toy. "Take Woody?"

"No. Woody has to stay here."

Kaliska looked around. "Mommy?"

"Mommy will stay where she is, Kaliska. She doesn't want to be with me." That assessment tripped off his human tongue without any problem. In truth he had no idea what was going on with Sara and it was too late to find out now. He hated who he became in this body. He shifted, waiting for his daughter to do the same. When she didn't, he turned back to Istaga. "Come on, Kaliska. We have to go now."

"No," she said, sticking out her lower lip and folding her chubby arms over her chest.

The blue-eyed stubborn stare, the frizzy sun hair surrounding her round face reminded Istaga so much of Sara that he let out a howl, scaring Kaliska in the process. With water pouring from his eyes he picked her up and carried her, hoping he could convince her to shift. Without that he had no way of feeding her.

An hour later Kaliska had fallen sound asleep in his arms. It was time to rest but he didn't feel safe sleeping out in the open with a small child. He was closer to the mountains now and decided to keep going for a while. Once he was higher up there was sure to be a cave where the two of them could seek shelter. Unfortunately these eastern mountains were unfamiliar to him.

It was less than an hour later that he came into a clearing in the middle of the forest. In front of him was an abandoned cabin, a dirt road leading down a hill on the other side. There were no tire tracks leading up to it and no sign of recent habitation, but before making up his mind he placed the sleeping child on the ground and shifted to Coyote. With his sensitive nose he could tell how recently humans had been here. His examination of the area around the house turned up nothing. It had been many months since anyone had come this way. He heaved his shoulder against the door to break the rusted lock, picked up the baby and headed inside.

He found canned goods in the kitchen area and water came out of the pipe when he turned the handle. Luckily Sara had taught him how to use the metal thing he found in a drawer to removed the tops of the cans. This was as good a place as any to hang out with Kaliska until he came up with a plan.

Istaga was dreaming, the whine of the mechanical

beast incorporated into his anticipation of Sara's arrival. He could almost smell her. He opened his arms, anticipating her body falling into them, and what they would do together when she did.

"You!" The voice woke him abruptly and when he opened his eyes he recognized the man who leaned over the bed.

He turned his head but Kaliska was not where he'd left her.

"Hey Bob, is this the guy from the mountain?" Raleigh called out loudly.

A second later another familiar face looked down. "That's him all right."

I should have killed him when I had the chance, Istaga thought to himself. When he tried to sit up Raleigh pushed him down. "You aren't going anywhere except to jail, unless we decide to kill you instead."

13

*S*ara headed into the mountains early the next morning. Without being able to shift it took her twice as long to get up to their former cave where she hoped to find them. But the place was abandoned with no sign that Istaga had been there anytime recently. She spent the night curled into the sleeping bag she'd brought along, her dreams filled with Istaga, his long hair hanging in her face as he made love to her. When she woke in the morning her face felt salty as though she'd cried in her sleep. She ate the trail mix she'd brought along, her thoughts scattering into the higher mountains where they'd taken refuge, but she couldn't remember how to get there. Without being able to shift it was useless to go on. She sat in the sun with her eyes closed, trying to stop the sobs that bubbled up, but finally she let them come, unchecked tears making their way down her already salty cheeks.

She arrived at Rosie's house in the wee hours of Monday morning and let herself into the house with her key. She slipped into the guest bedroom as quietly as she could, trying to let go of the desperate feeling that kept her from sleeping.

"You're back!" Rosie said when she dragged herself out for coffee the next morning. "Didn't find them, I take it."

Sara shook her head, accepting the cup Rosie handed her. "If I could shift I know I could find them," she mumbled between sips.

"He'll be back," Rosie assured her. "He loves you."

After Rosie left she showered and dragged herself to work. Until she formed a plan there was nothing she could do but hope Istaga would realize what he was doing. He had loved her once; surely he couldn't be this cruel. But then a niggling thought would enter her mind that maybe it hadn't been Istaga who kidnapped her baby. But if not him, then who?

"You look like something the cat dragged in," Joe commented when she entered the kitchen.

"I feel like it too."

"What did you do—go on a weekend bender?"

"No, Joe. My baby was kidnapped on Friday. I haven't slept since."

"My god, Sunny. Why are you here?"

"I can't do anything about it. At least here I can keep my mind off it for a while."

"What do the police say?"

Sara looked up from where she was tying on her apron. "I couldn't tell them."

Joe stared at her without speaking and then finally asked, "Why not?"

Sara sighed, fatigue settling into her limbs. "It's a long story that I'd rather not get into."

"If you're wanted by the law, I..."

"I'm fired?" She stared at him defiantly.

"What did you do, if you don't mind my asking?"

"I didn't do anything, that's the point. My husband

is framing me and has been for several years."

"Sunny, I like you. You're a good worker. But I don't know if I can continue with this arrangement. You know the cops from Black Base come in here all the time. I don't want to get in the middle of something."

"They don't know me from Adam. I dyed my hair and besides, it's longer now."

"Jesus, Mary and Joseph," Joe said, running his hands through his thick graying hair. He shook his head and turned back to the stove where hash browns were frying.

Sara tightened her apron and went into the other room to set up. The café was due to open in ten minutes.

❧

Days had gone by with no sign of Istaga or Kaliska. Sara couldn't sleep and barely ate, her mind constantly whirling with some way to find her baby.

"Sara, you really need to rest! If you don't you're going to end up in the hospital. Have you looked at yourself lately?"

"Would you sleep if your baby was missing, Rosie? I don't know what to do. I can't go to the police and I don't even know for sure who took her."

"I'm going over to the Pig and Pint and see if anyone knows anything. John seems to be a fount of information—maybe's he's heard something. I'm still betting on Istaga."

"Hurry back!" Sara called as Rosie slipped out the door.

After the truck roared to life and rumbled away Sara went to the cabinet over the sink and pulled out the bottle of tequila. She got a glass from the drainer and carried both over to the table. Her breasts were so painful she felt like screaming and every ache brought her thoughts to her missing baby. She tipped the glass of liquid into her mouth, swallowed and poured another.

∽⧢⧢

"Sara, Sara! Wake up!"

Sara opened her eyes, blearily taking in Rosie's worried expression. At some point she'd moved to the couch although she had no memory of it.

"What did you do, drink the entire bottle? Jesus, Sara, what am I going to do with you?"

"It numbs the pain and it put me to sleep," she slurred, trying to sit up. "What did you find out?"

Rosie sighed and made a face. "Raleigh's in Black Base but I doubt very seriously that he took Kaliska. He arrived Sunday night, and from what I heard from John he was heading up to his cabin."

"John seems to be our local news guy, doesn't he?"

"Don't be too hard on him. He's concerned about you."

"Oh please. The only person John's concerned about is himself. I hope you didn't tell him about Kaliska."

Rosie frowned. "You expected me to keep it a secret? John won't tell anybody. And I'm sure he can help us find her."

Sara slumped sideways and began to cry. "I don't want anybody to know!" she wailed. "Kaliska is a shifter. If they find her...oh Jesus..."

Rosie sat down next to her. "I think you should tell him the truth."

"Tell John that my mate is really a coyote and that we had a half coyote baby and that my baby, who might or might not be in coyote form, has been kidnapped? I don't think so."

"I admit he can be a jerk but he's not really such a bad guy. And he has a four wheel drive truck, a gun and tracking abilities."

The conversation had sobered Sara up. "Since when did you become such a John fan? No, Rosie. We have to come up with another way."

"I don't know any other way and neither do you. You need help with this and John's our best bet."

"I'll sleep on it," Sara finally agreed.

14

$\mathcal{R}$aleigh and his friend Bob tied Istaga's hands behind his back with heavy rope and then dragged him from the cabin and threw him into the back of the pick-up. As Raleigh backed up and pulled away Istaga scanned for Kaliska but there was no sign of her. He nearly called out but if Raleigh found out she was with him he hated to think what might happen. Hopefully she'd shifted and taken off. As a coyote she was fine on her own, old enough to hunt and old enough to find a mate. But as a baby…his heart gave an uneven thump as he contemplated what would happen to her. Many predators would be very happy to dine on a succulent little human that plump.

The truck bumped and careened down the hill, bruising him as he was thrown from side to side. Without the use of his hands he was helpless. He thought once about shifting but figured he'd be tied up as a coyote as well. No point in it.

Once they reached town the ride became smoother but this did nothing to help his mood. They were not arriving in Black Base—this was a larger town that he didn't recognize. At the police station Bob and Raleigh took hold of his arms and marched him inside.

"This is the man I reported a few months back," Raleigh told the cop behind the desk. "He nearly killed my friend here," he added, gesturing to Bob.

"Yeah, he was at my throat, but the worst thing was what he…"

Raleigh put a restraining hand on Bob's arm, giving him a warning look. Apparently they didn't want to mention the shifting.

"At your throat?" the cop at the counter asked with a puzzled expression, pausing with his pen in the air.

"Yeah, you know," Raleigh said quickly. "He had his hands around Bob's neck. Would have strangled him if it hadn't been for Bob's buddy. This bastard also stole Bob's guns."

Istaga tuned out as the cops whispered amongst themselves while they searched through reports.

"Is this the shifter?" one finally asked, pulling out a piece of paper with a grainy photo on it and trying not to laugh.

Raleigh turned beet red. "He's a psychopath and needs to be behind bars. Do you have any idea who I am?"

"I don't really care who you are," the cop said, turning away again. He talked to the other cop for a while and then went into an office.

A few minutes later another man joined them and this one seemed to be in charge. "We'll stick him in a cell and take your statement, but I'm not sure what the problem is."

"He was in my cabin, sleeping in my bed!" Raleigh yelled. "He broke in and he's dangerous! You'd know all about this guy if you ever took the time to watch the news. It was when the hunters were here."

The cop narrowed his eyes, obviously irritated by Raleigh's patronizing tone. "Someone had a lot of fun with that video," he said. The other cops chuckled.

Raleigh looked ready to punch someone but somehow restrained himself. "He's a criminal and I'll prove it to you."

"Okay, Buddy, you do that. I can only hold him for forty-eight hours."

One of the cops led Istaga down a hall and into a holding cell. He untied his hands and slid the barred door closed and locked it. "Don't go anywhere," he said, grinning.

Istaga gazed around at the box he was in. In the corner was a water-filled bowl where he could let his water go, and along the wall a piece of flat metal jutted out that he figured was a place to sit or lie down. On the far wall was a sink. There was no window and the stench of fear, piss and sweat made him gag.

He paced up and down, feeling like he might explode before he remembered the words Sara had taught him: *Om Mani Padme Hum.* He couldn't remember what she'd told him it meant, only that saying it was very calming to the nervous system. After five minutes of repeating the four words he had at least given up the idea of turning into a coyote and howling at the moon.

He unzipped his jeans and pissed into the water, watching it mix with the sky color, turning it the color of fresh weeds that appeared after the rains. He shook his head wondering what that indicated. Did it measure or show something that was particular to him?

Hopefully it wouldn't reveal his true identity. He crouched on the floor and tried not to think about Kaliska and what might be happening to her. If only he could contact Sara.

"Okay, bud," he heard someone say.

Istaga sat up from where he'd been dozing against the wall.

"If you have anyone you want to call you'd better do it now. That Raleigh guy wants to throw the book at you. Personally I don't like him and I think what's he's saying is a bunch of bullshit."

Istaga stared, trying to make sense of the words. "I know a female, my mate," he said, standing. "But I don't know how to reach her."

"Where does she live?"

"Black Base. She has a friend called Rosie. Maybe she's with her."

"Rosie Airs?"

Istaga shrugged. "I don't know."

"What's your wife's name?"

"Wife? Sara is my mate. She has sun hair and sky eyes and she comes to here." He held his hand out to indicate where Sara came up to on him, which was around his chin.

"Okay, I'll admit you're weird. Sun hair I suppose means blonde? Blue eyes? I'll give the Rosie I know a call. Maybe you'll get lucky." The guy chuckled before leaving Istaga alone again.

Istaga was dreaming of Raven and feeling terrible under the bird's harsh scrutiny. He hadn't done what the bird had told him to do and now Raven was furious with him. In the midst of this he heard a familiar voice say his name. His eyes blinked open.

"Sara?" he said, nearly falling in his haste to stand. She was on the other side of the bars, her worried expression making his heart pound. And then the water came and he couldn't stop it from pouring down his cheeks.

"What happened to your hair?" he asked, trying to touch it through the bars.

"I dyed it again," she said. "I was trying to keep under Raleigh's radar but what you did put both of us in his cross hairs."

Istaga was too involved with staring at her to comment. She looked different, as though her eyes had been bruised in some way. Her skin seemed too tight across her cheekbones. There was a hollowness about her that made him ache inside.

"They're releasing you into my custody. I can't fathom why, since Raleigh has filed charges against you that could keep you in jail for a very long time. He wants to charge you with attempted murder. I guess that one cop felt sorry for you or something. He's at least part Native American so maybe he felt a kinship of some kind."

At that moment the cop entered the cell area and unlocked the door. "I expect you to stay around, Istaga. If Raleigh comes up with anything that sticks we'll need to interrogate you. Just be very glad that Rosie and I are friends. If it wasn't for her god knows what would happen to you. The system is hard to get out of once you're in it and without any identification you look like an illegal."

Focused only on Sara, Istaga had no idea what the man was saying. He wanted to take her in his arms but there was an invisible wall between them. He'd felt this before but had always managed to break through. This one was different.

When he followed her out to the truck and climbed in next to her she refused to meet his eyes. "What has happened?" he finally asked once they were headed down the road. And then he thought of Kaliska. Sara must be imagining a helpless baby wandering around alone. Or did she even know?

"Our baby is gone," she finally answered without taking her eyes off the road.

"I know."

"You know?" she swiveled toward him, her eyes wild. "I thought...did you take her?" Sara pulled the truck off the road, spraying gravel in her haste to bring it to a stop.

Istaga nodded and then reached for her hand but she shrank away from him.

"Where is she?"

"We were staying in Raleigh's cabin. We had food and I decided to wait there until she would agree to shift. But when I woke up she was gone. She's a coyote, Sara. She is old enough to be on her own."

"Are you telling me you left her there?"

"What choice did I have? Raleigh and Bob tied me up and brought me down here to jail."

"Do they know?"

Istaga shook his head. "If Kaliska was toddling

around outside that cabin I would have known. She took off before Bob and Raleigh got there. Maybe she could hear the mechanical beast coming? She refused to shift before that."

When Sara stared out the window Istaga could see water shining on her cheeks. She put the truck into gear and moved back onto the road without saying another word.

15

*S*ara couldn't think straight. Seeing Istaga again was bad enough but having her only child lost up in the mountains was too much. And his blasé way of talking about their baby, like she was mostly coyote, was infuriating. Kaliska was human. The only time she shifted now was when they put her in her pen. What did she know of living on her own or coyote packs and mates?

She couldn't even look at Istaga without wanting to strangle him. Why had he stayed away all this time, and why in god's name hadn't he waited for her instead of stealing their child and heading into the mountains? She hated him right now and the only reason she'd agreed to take him was because she knew what would happen if she didn't. If the inmates didn't kill him, he'd shift and kill one of them. Jail was not the place for Istaga.

At Rosie's house she parked and got out, leaving Istaga sitting there. If he took off right now it was fine with her. But he was right on her heels as she went through the door.

The expression on Rosie's face when Istaga followed her inside was somewhere between shock and disbelief, her gaze going from one to the other.

"He's in my custody," Sara told her, before heading

to the fridge for a beer. "And Kaliska is up in the mountains alone. " She shot Istaga a look and then sat down at the table.

"So it *was* you," Rosie said. "Do you want a beer?" she asked Istaga, heading for the fridge.

Istaga nodded. He sat on the couch and put his head in his hands.

"Don't try to gain my sympathy, Istaga," Sara said sharply, watching him. "I'll never forgive you for this." When she said these words something in her chest turned over, as though her body had a very different way of looking at things. She had a perfect right to be furious, didn't she? Just the fear about her child was enough to turn her into a raving lunatic. "What are we going to do about Kaliska? Any ideas, Coyote-man?"

Istaga looked up, his eyes bleak. "I told you what I think. She is coyote. And if she shifts back she will know soon enough that being coyote is a lot safer."

"She's only two years old!"

Istaga shook his head and looked down. "No, Sara. She's nearly full-grown. Her instincts will kick in."

Sara slugged down the rest of her beer and went to get another. "I'm going to find John and ask him to help me track her. I can't leave her out there. And besides, I want my baby back! To hell with her coyote life—she's my baby and I love her."

"Sara, I'm sorry…"

"Don't bother," Sara interrupted. "You haven't searched us out all these months and then you come by and steal our child away? What exactly did you expect?"

"I was afraid…I was…"

"Spare me the drama, Istaga," Sara answered. "I don't want to hear your sob story."

"Sara, you should at least hear him out," Rosie interjected, handing Istaga a bottle of beer.

Sara shook her head and slammed her half-full bottle down on the table, spraying foam over the wood. "I'm going to the Pig and Pint," she announced, heading for the door. "And please, don't come after me!"

She opened the door and was slamming it shut when Istaga pushed though the opening. "If anyone can track our child it is me!" he yelled, the door banging against the outside wall. He grabbed her arm and swung her around.

"Let me go!"

She pulled away but he grabbed her again, his yellow eyes narrowed and menacing. "You are not telling John about Kaliska or asking for his help. I am her sire and it is my responsibility to find her."

When Sara met his gaze she knew there was no arguing with him. "If Raleigh finds you anywhere near his cabin again he'll either shoot you or have the authorities all over you."

"I do not give a fuck, Sara. This is Kaliska we are talking about. Now get in the fucking truck and drive."

Sara's nerves were strung so tight she was on the edge of hysteria. A second later she was doubled over, laughing out of control.

"What the fuck?" he said, watching her.

"It's that word, Istaga," she said, trying to gulp in

air. "It gets me every time."

Sara tried to count all the different parts of speech Istaga had just employed, but she couldn't stop laughing.

✖✖

Once she got herself under control, Sara joined Istaga in Rosie's truck, sliding behind the steering wheel. She drove out of town, heading east toward the mountain range while Istaga navigated, pointing out the narrow dirt road that led up the hill toward the cabin. It took nearly two hours to get there because of the recent monsoon downpour, which had rutted out the road and left deep puddles behind. The rains had come early this year. Rosie's vintage truck whined in protest as the hill grew steeper.

"Park here," Istaga finally ordered, pointing out a narrow cutoff that led beneath trees. "It is a good place to hide the mechanical beast."

Sara drove as far as she could until branches began to scrape against the cab roof. She pulled to a stop and cut the motor. "How far is the cabin?"

"Not far."

Istaga didn't think in hours or minutes. 'Not far' for him could mean anywhere between a half hour and two hours. She looked at him now, noticing for the first time how hollow he seemed. His black hair had grown and was tangled into dreadlocks. He was thinner than she remembered and his shoulders were rolled forward as though he carried something heavy on his back. "I'm sorry I blamed you," she began cautiously. "It's been so long--why didn't you come find us? You must have known where we were."

When Istaga turned she could clearly see the pain in his eyes. "I've had my own things to take care of, Sara. I've been doing what we planned—trying to warn the animals about the hunters. There was a fire up there that wiped out our old shelter and burned half the forest down. Animals were caught up in it and many died."

"What about the rumors I've been hearing? Did you nearly kill someone?"

Istaga looked away. "I wish I had killed him. He had it coming." He shook his head and focused on his hands. "He pushed me too far."

"Everyone's talking about it and now Raleigh has even more fuel for his fire."

"Fuck Raleigh." Istaga opened the door and jumped out, waiting for her to do the same.

Sara pulled the keys out of the ignition and stuffed them in her pocket before creaking her door open and sliding out. "Lead the way."

He eyed her for a moment and then shifted, heading up the road away from her.

"Wait!" she called out. "I can't shift!"

Coyote turned, his ears pricked forward. A moment later Istaga stood in his place. "What do you mean you can't shift?"

"I can't shift anymore. I've tried a zillion times—I just tried again."

"How do you plan to track Kaliska?"

"Humans can track."

Istaga narrowed his gaze and shook his head. "Not like coyotes. Shall I leave you here?"

Sara's chest felt tight. "Go. I'll follow on foot as fast as I can. I'll call to her—maybe she's in human form."

"Do not make noise, Sara. If anyone is around they will come after us."

"Then how can I help?"

Istaga watched her for a moment in silence before he shifted and loped quickly up the hill away from her.

Sara stood there for a full minute before she moved under the trees to search out an animal trail that led upward. When tears welled she wiped them away—in the three years they'd known each other she'd never felt this disconnected from Istaga.

Sara came upon the cabin an hour later. She waited under the trees, listening for any sounds before she snuck around the side. The door was locked but around back a window had been pushed open enough to crawl through. She squeezed through into a bathroom, lowered herself to the floor and went to check the rest of the cabin.

Before she reached the bedroom/living room she heard the howl of a coyote, recognizing Istaga/Coyote's call. From within the cabin another answering howl pierced the air—high-pitched and scared. Sara hurtled through the doorway to see Kaliska in animal form sitting on the bed with her ears pricked listening.

"Kaliska!" When Sara hurried toward her the young coyote jumped off the bed and ran by, heading for the open window.

Sara took off after her, falling out the window in

her haste to keep the coyote in sight. She was struggling to stand when she saw Kaliska disappear under the trees. *If only I could shift,* she agonized, but she couldn't and she had to track her baby on foot. Hopefully once Kaliska found her father, Istaga would come and find Sara. If he didn't she didn't know what she'd do.

She jogged as quickly as she could, following a meandering trail that she hoped was where Kaliska had gone. She put her hands around her mouth and tried to howl but the sound that came out was pathetic and only loud enough to reach her immediate area.

She sped up, heading further into the forest , sure she saw Kaliska's bushy tail disappearing around a bend, but when she reached the place where the trail curved to the left Kaliska was no longer in sight. When another trail intersected the one she was on she put her nose to the ground trying to determine which way Kaliska had chosen, but her human senses did not pick up what she needed and there were no fresh prints. She decided on the wider of the two trails and scrambled up what was fast becoming too steep for her two-legged form. Again she thought the thoughts that always brought her into coyote form, and again nothing happened.

Sara stopped for a moment to catch her breath, scanning the rocky trail ahead of her and where it led. It was bare of vegetation with rocks ranging from pebble size to boulders, and many were loose. She would never make it up those steep sides. Already her feet had slipped and caused minor slides. Instead of continuing she decided to backtrack and take the less steep way up. Once she was on the ridge she would surely find her mate and her baby.

At some point she realized that she was completely lost. Too many trail turnings and picking between them without paying attention. The ridge was still far above her and it was growing dark. "Istaga!" she shouted, putting her hands around her mouth. Listening brought only the sigh of wind through the high tree branches, and the rustle of small creatures around her. She continued on.

It was dense night by the time Sara decided she had to stop. The ridge was still a misty vision in the distance through the moonlight—it felt like she would never reach it. She could barely breathe at this altitude and her lungs were on fire from her helter skelter climb. She pulled herself into a shallow opening in the rock face, hugged her arms around her shivering body and fell asleep.

Sara stared at the beautiful red tail hawk perched on a stone at the edge of a pool of dark water. He was larger than any hawk she'd ever seen, his wings tipped in gold. She looked around and didn't recognize where she was. Hadn't she fallen asleep in a shallow cave? She was now in a clearing surrounded with dark trees--sentinels that seemed to breathe in and out in a sort of sleepy rhythm. The pool was inviting, surrounded with smooth river stones, water stained silver where the moonlight touched it. This had to be a dream. "I'm trying to find Istaga and my baby," she answered. "Can you help me?"

"To find your mate and your chick you must delve deep

inside and discover why it is that your heart has turned cold."

"My heart's not cold. I love Kaliska."

The hawk turned his head, fixing her with one bright amber eye. "What of your mate?"

"I..." Sara paused, wondering why she couldn't say the words. "He left me. He didn't look for me."

The hawk blinked and shook out its feathers. "Who left?" he asked, the question hanging in the air like an accusation.

Sara looked away, wondering why this question upset her so much. Was all of this her fault? But it was Istaga who had taken off first. She'd only come down to Black Base because he was gone. She thought back to that flight down the mountain, her rush to bring her baby into town. She hadn't given it a second thought, hadn't considered how Istaga would feel when he got back and the two of them were gone. A sick feeling rolled through her.

When she looked at the hawk again he seemed to nod. "You understand now."

"I took his baby away?" she asked. Was this her biggest sin?

"That is only part of it. You have much to make up for, Sara."

It was very strange to hear her name come out of the bird's mouth. "How do I find them?"

But the hawk already had his wings spread and a second later lifted into the night sky, turning into a dark shadow as it flew away. Sara moved to the pool and gazed into the water where an image was forming. She gasped when she saw Istaga looking back at her, Kaliska in his arms. "Where are you?" she cried out, but he didn't answer and a second later the water swirled and turned black without even a shred of moonlight to lighten its surface. When she looked up the moon was gone and all she could see were stars, billions of them. They seemed to mock her as they blinked on and off.

Sara woke in her little shelter, the dream world still very much with her. There were messages here, things she had to think about, but already the wisps of the dream were dissipating. She shivered remembering the bird's message. What did the hawk mean, 'she had much to make up for'? What had *she* done? It was Istaga who was at fault. He should have understood her need to be with her own kind.

Sara brushed herself off and headed back to the little trail, working her way upward as dawn broke. She stopped for a moment to watch the gray sky turn pink and then magenta, a sign that a storm might be coming. Why she felt compelled to reach the ridge was not something she understood, it was like her coyote instincts had kicked in, propelling her higher and higher.

❦

The sun was high when Sara finally reached the top, but there were clouds on the horizon and they were moving in her direction. A brisk breeze had begun and she wrapped her arms around her body, wishing she'd thought to bring a jacket. From here she had a view of the distant mountains rolling downward, valley upon valley drifting into shadow. Mists obscured the higher peaks that lay to the east. And in between were vast forests that lay dark and impenetrable. That was where she was sure she would find them. But would they still be there by the time she reached those trees?

A shot rang out and then another sending her scurrying behind a tree. She crouched, wondering if they were aiming at her. For all she knew it could be Raleigh up here. A second later another shot boomed across the silence, the sound making the hair on her arms stand up.

Sara jumped when a hand clamped down on her shoulder, a voice hissing in her ear. "What are you doing up here?"

Sara turned, staring into the face of a man dressed in camouflage with a gun slung across his shoulder. "I..."

"You could have been shot. Don't you know it's hunting season?" He laughed. "Up here it's always hunting season." He looked her up and down. "You could be mistaken for a deer with that hair of yours." He took hold of her arm and hauled her to her feet. "Better come with me. We'll keep you safe."

Sara wrenched away from him. "I don't want to come with..."

He clamped a heavy hand over her mouth and twisted her arms behind her back. "You'll do exactly what I tell you to do." He pulled a length of rope out of his pocket and tied her wrists together before pushing her ahead of him down the trail.

Sara stumbled across rocks, trying to remain upright, her mind unable to come to grips with what had happened. "What do you want with me?" she asked, but he didn't answer.

After walking for about ten minutes they arrived at a clearing where three other men sat hunched around a campfire. Her captor gave Sara a shove and she fell to her knees. "Look what I found," he announced. "Weren't you guys talking about needing a woman?" He let out a nasty laugh. "Maybe she can cook too."

He grabbed Sara and undid her hands and then looped a rope around her neck while the other men eyed her suspiciously.

Two of them looked to be in their early twenties, the other one in his late forties, the same age as her captor. They appeared to have been out in the woods for a while, with dirty beards and caked mud on their boots, filthy hair and a stench of sweat. Maybe they were survivalists or something. A deer carcass had been strung up on a rack to dry and there were buckets of water for washing as well as several sleeping bags. Sara sat down on a log and tried not to let her fear show as she listened to their conversation.

"There's a coyote hanging around here," one of the younger ones said. "I heard him last night."

"Yeah, I heard him too. We need to track the bastard and shoot him."

Sara felt a shiver as she imagined Istaga and Kaliska. He would be easy prey in his present vulnerable state. "Why do you kill coyotes? You can't eat them."

"Do you know how much their pelts are worth?" one of them asked her.

She shook her head and looked at the ground.

"I don't know either but I do know it's a good chunk of change."

Not long after that declaration, her captor tied her up again, this time securing her legs as well. The four men picked up their guns and left camp and a short time later she heard gunfire in the distance. She held her breath, praying to the universe that they weren't after Istaga and Kaliska.

Sara worked at her bound arms and legs but before she could loosen the ropes the men trooped back into camp. She breathed a sigh of relief when she saw they were empty-handed. But not being able to kill anything had brought up frustration and anger, and when one of them produced a bottle of whiskey they began to pass it around. Sara watched them nervously as they eyed her in more than a friendly manner. When one of them rose from the log and headed toward her, she shrank back.

"Almost time for you to earn your keep," he slurred, grinning slyly.

He untied her and looped the rope around her neck, pulling her to sit next to him. He offered her a drink but she shook her head. By now the bottle was nearly empty and moods had begun to turn dark. All the men were focusing on her as though she was to be the next entertainment.

"I say we take turns," one of the younger guys said, staring at her avidly. "We can draw straws to see who goes first."

Sara swallowed down the bile that rose in her throat. She was strong but not strong enough. The man next to her, who was broad chested and muscly, turned to the other one. "I'm first and if you don't like it try and stop me." He stood, waiting for one of the others to challenge him, but no one said a word. A moment later she was lurched to her feet, stumbling after him.

Sara tried to pull away, hoping that in his drunken state he didn't have a good grip on the rope, but she was wrong. He reached a spot under the trees and pushed her to the ground. "This can go one of two ways," he said, pulling a pistol out of his belt. "Either you cooperate or I kill you. Now take off your clothes."

Sara didn't have to think twice about unbuttoning her shirt. Before she had her jeans completely off he took hold of the rope and dragged her toward him. When she kicked out, catching him in the groin, he let out a high-pitched scream, but before she could escape he was on top of her and had her pinned. She screamed as loud as she could and kept on screaming.

What happened next was so surreal she wondered if she might be dreaming. An enormous coyote leapt out from under the trees and went for the man's neck. It was only a minute before the man gurgled his last breath and his lifeless body rolled off her. When Sara rolled away and looked at him blood was pouring from the enormous gash in his neck, his eyes still open and staring at nothing.

She was on her knees retching into the weeds when the other three men appeared. One of them had a handgun pointed straight at the coyote, but before he pulled the trigger Sara moved forward and grabbed it out of his hand. She threw it as far as she could, watching in shock as Coyote lunged for him. The man let out a shriek, his large body slamming against the ground as the animal bit into him. "No!" she screamed. "Don't kill him!" The coyote turned, his yellow eyes meeting hers. His teeth were red with blood. When she looked down at the man his eyes had glazed over, but he was still breathing. The other two men seemed frozen as they watched the scene, but a second later one of them retrieved the gun and shots rang out.

Sara closed her eyes, afraid to see what was happening, but a half a minute later Istaga removed the rope from her neck and grabbed her hand, heading into the dense brush. When she looked back two men were running away and the other was on the ground bleeding from a wound in his chest. How had that happened?

Sara felt like she was dreaming, her feet barely touching the ground as she ran after Istaga. Was this some elaborate hallucination like her weird dream about the hawk? But when Istaga finally stopped and his eyes met hers she knew this was very real. "You are hurt," he said, staring at the bleeding cuts and scratches on her arms and legs.

Sara looked down, surprised to see that she didn't have a stitch on. She barely remembered anything from the moment the man dragged her away from camp. "Not as hurt as I would have been if you hadn't happened along."

Istaga took off his shirt and helped her put it on. When he pulled her into his arms she sobbed until there were no more tears, feeling his fingers working through her hair, his lips against her cheek. When he kissed her she kissed him back, all her anger forgotten in her relief to be alive.

16

"Where did you leave Kaliska?" Sara asked, following Istaga down a narrow trail. She figured he was taking her to wherever he'd left their baby, anticipation filling her with adrenaline. Her need for comforting had lasted longer than it should have and now all she wanted was to be reunited with Kaliska, to feed her and stop the ache from her over full breasts. She imagined the feel of her soft baby hair against her skin, her baby smell, the pleasurable sensations that came with providing her baby with sustenance.

Istaga turned, his level gaze meeting hers. "Our coyote pup is long gone, Sara. She took off right after she found me in the woods. I think she's found a mate."

"That can't be! She's just a baby!"

"I told you before that she is not a baby, she is nearly grown. This is her decision."

"Why did you let her go?" Sara demanded, heat coursing through her in an angry wave.

"I could not stop her. And she refused to shift."

"When I found her in the cabin she heard your call and took off. She didn't even look at me."

Istaga gathered his loose hair into a ponytail and tied it back, his gaze going into the distance. "This was the chance we took having offspring. She has decided that her destiny lies with animals, not humans."

"How do you know that?"

"Sara, she is gone. I'm not sure I could even track her now."

Sara stopped in the middle of the trail, her chest heaving as she tried not to cry. "Did she really find a pack?"

"I heard them in the woods and she did too. She went after them."

"Is this what happens?" Sara asked, collapsing onto the ground. "My two- year-old takes off and I never see her again?" She put her head in her hands and began to cry.

Istaga crouched next to her. "Kaliska is nearly three now, old enough to be on her own. I tried to talk to you about it. We went hunting together. This is what coyotes do. "

"But I want my baby back! She was still breast-feeding! How can this be?"

When Istaga placed his hand on her arm she shook it off. "This is all your fault. You should have brought her back to me. You shouldn't have let her spend so much time as a coyote." Sara looked over at him her mind going to the horrific scene they had just left. "And you killed a man back there! How could you do that?" she wailed.

Istaga held her gaze. "You were in trouble."

"You could have stopped him without killing him-- now you're a murderer!" Sara yelled.

"I did what I knew to save you. Those are bad men and they were hunting where it is not allowed. They would have harmed you."

Istaga stared at her for a long moment after he said these words, his face expressionless. When he stood and walked away Sara watched him go, his two-legged body changing seamlessly into Coyote. The animal melted into the brush as though he'd never been there. She didn't call after him, didn't try and stop him. All she felt was a searing anger that took up all the space inside her. She could barely breathe.

She sat there for a long time letting the tears stream down her face before she decided to check on the man who had been shot. Perhaps he was still alive and she could help him. But when she backtracked and reached the spot where the massacre had taken place a large mountain lion and two nearly full-grown cubs were feeding. And from the mess it was obvious the second man was as dead as the first one. Sara backed away as quietly as she could and then retched into the bushes until there was nothing left to bring up.

She took off down the hill, trying to get the horrible images out of her mind but they kept replaying over and over, the horror of it making her run faster until she was falling every couple of steps, her knees bleeding and bruised from the falls. Istaga was gone, her baby was gone, and four men had nearly raped her. It began to rain, making her trip down the increasingly slick paths even more difficult. She was frantic with worry and sick at heart about her baby and unsure of the route she should be on, but somehow she kept going.

❦

"My god, Sara! What happened up there?" Rosie led Sara to the couch and pushed her gently down before heading to the sink for warm water and soap. "Whose shirt is that and where are your clothes?"

Sara put her head back and closed her eyes. "He killed a man, Rosie. And my baby is gone. She's a coyote now and I'll never see her again."

Rosie returned and began to gently wash the cuts on Sara's arms and legs. "You don't know that."

Sara let out a long sigh. "Why would she return? According to Istaga she's found a mate." Sara began to cry. "I wish I'd never met him!"

"Don't say that. You love each other. Who could have predicted this?"

"Istaga said he knew she would choose coyote over being human." Sara took the tissue Rosie held out and wiped her eyes and then blew her nose. "What am I going to do?"

Rosie pressed her lips together. "First of all you're going to clean yourself up and call your boss. He's called at least five times to check on you. And then you're going to eat a decent meal. You need food and rest and then we'll talk again in the morning."

Sara called Joe and tried to explain why she hadn't shown up for work for the past few days.

"Have you found your child?" he asked.

"No, Joe. She's still out there somewhere."

There was silence and then Joe said, "You need to get the police on this, Sunny. Do that and then get your butt back to work. It won't do you any good to mope around and besides, I need you."

"That man has the patience of Job," Rosie remarked after Sara explained the conversation.

"He can't get good help up there. He's tried but they always quit after a day or two."

"Eat," Rosie said, handing her a plate of tortillas, meat, beans, and salad. "And then take a bath and go to bed."

≈≈

Sara lay back in the claw foot tub, all her cuts and scrapes stinging from the hot water. When she closed her eyes she saw the man on top of, felt the terror all over again. Just another minute and things would have turned out very differently. She shuddered, the reality of it what had nearly happened penetrating into her brain for the first time. There had been three others waiting their turn.

The vision of Coyote attacking appeared in her mind, the blood everywhere, and the horrible sound of gurgling as he tried to suck in air through his severed windpipe. She opened her eyes, focusing on the towel rack, the flower printed wallpaper and the steam that covered the mirror. She was here and safe. But then she remembered her daughter and let out a sob.

"What's the matter?" Rosie cried, opening the bathroom door.

"Nothing, just all of it."

Rosie came over and looked down on her. "You're a mess, Sara. And I don't know what to do for you because you haven't told me everything that happened up there." She shook her head. "Going back to work is probably the best thing for now. Do you want a sleeping pill?"

Sara looked up gratefully. "Do you have something?"

Rosie nodded. "For emergencies only." She went to the medicine cabinet and pulled out a prescription bottle. "Ambien. I got it a year ago when I was going through some weird stuff that seemed related to my hormonal levels. Anyway there's nearly a full bottle here." She placed it next to the sink. "At least you'll sleep."

17

*C*oyote pricked his ears, trying to decipher the distant coyote calls. Was that Kaliska's voice he heard? It sounded more like a wolf than a coyote. He'd heard of these half-breeds that had moved into the mountains. Their offspring were larger and more able to defend against other animals. His coyote brain knew the wolves were breeding with coyotes because their own kind had been driven to near extinction.

His mind was muddled and he struggled to get control of his senses. He lifted his nose into the wind, letting the scents come to him, one by one. There was a skunk somewhere close, something dead not too far away and there was the pack that he could hear over the next ridge. He headed in that direction, dimly aware of some need to find his offspring.

He was very far from the place he'd last seen his mate. His body felt weak and he didn't know why. He'd had to bring up the contents of his stomach several times in the past few days and the smell of blood now made him sick. When he saw a rabbit run by, his first instinct was to go after it, but a second later the image of the raw meat and the blood had him retching again. He curled into a ball and slept.

When he woke again he was Istaga, his thoughts going to his last conversation with Sara. She blamed him for Kaliska's disappearance. He should never have taken Kaliska out of Rosie's house. If he hadn't none of this would have happened. There was water on his face, water that he couldn't stop from coming out of his eyes. He let out a strangled cry that echoed across the valley. A second later his stomach convulsed and he was retching again. Why was this happening? He hadn't eaten in many turnings of the sun and his body was weak and shaky. But every time he thought of meat he couldn't stand it, the memory of the smell turning his stomach into painful knots.

His mind went to Sara and what had nearly happened to her. He couldn't understand the ways of men, how they used their strength to overpower the females of their species. Why was Sara angry with him for saving her? If he hadn't heard her screams all four would have hurt her. And from what he knew about men of this sort, they would have killed her once they were finished with her.

He wished he had never met Sara. The gift from the *was'ichu,* who claimed to be a shaman, had only caused him pain. And now he and Sara had brought a pup into the world--another source of conflict between them. Sara wanted a human baby and Istaga wanted Kaliska to be free and coyote.

If only he had listened to Raven's advice. The bird had told him over and over how foolish he was to fall in love with a human woman. He should have stuck with his pack and never looked back. But it was too late now. This ill-fated love had brought him to this point in his life—a point where he had to make a decision.

Should he leave the human part of him behind? If he did he could follow Kaliska and be with her and the pack she'd chosen. And yet when these thoughts went through his mind he felt an ache in the middle of his chest. What was life without Sara? But there was so much pain between them. He couldn't please her no matter what he did.

He gazed at the distant ridges stacked one after the other and leading into Mexico. He and Sara had lived in those mountains, had denned and brought Kaliska into the world. Sara had been happy during those early days, her laughter ringing across the rocky hills. They had loved each other deep in the night with Kaliska lying close beside them, their days spent playing with their pup and hunting for their dinner. She hadn't needed the company of humans back then. What had happened to change her?

When he sniffed the air he could almost smell the pinesap from those deep forests, the scent pulling at him. Soon the frozen water would fall, covering everything and changing the landscape. The word lonely came to him but he wasn't sure what it meant. It must have something to do with the hollow sensation he always carried in his belly and chest.

It was another two turnings of the sun before he reached a small town. He had no idea where he was but he figured he was close to the Mexican border. He had no money, no way to buy food, and nothing of value to trade now that his beads were gone. He lurched into a small café and sat down at the counter.

"What'll it be?"

"I have no money but I am hungry."

The sandy-haired man seemed familiar to Istaga but he was pretty sure he'd never met him before.

"Do you want a job?" the man asked. "My dishwasher just walked out."

Istaga wasn't sure what this job entailed but he nodded anyway, his mouth watering at the idea of food. "Can I eat first?"

"Sure. What do you want?"

"Something that is not meat."

"How about a bean and cheese burrito?"

Istaga shrugged. "Sure."

When the plate arrived Istaga put his nose close to sniff. When he didn't detect the smell of blood he bit into it and then chomped it down, licking his fingers after it was gone.

After the meal the manager, whose name was Ramon, took him in back and showed him the sink.

Istaga stared at the stacked dishes, the water that dripped from the metal bar that arced over the sink. What was he supposed to do?

"You have washed dishes, before, haven't you?" Ramon asked.

Istaga shrugged, turning toward him. "Not really."

Ramon let out a sigh before turning on the water and demonstrating. "Not difficult," he said, placing a plate in the drainer. "Think you can handle it?"

Istaga set to work and after ten minutes or so he got into the rhythm of things, enjoying the soapy warm water on his hands, the swipe with the sponge and quick rinse before he added each dish to the drainer. Loading the dishwasher was another matter and he despaired of ever getting it right, but somehow he filled the box, loading plates and pots into the network of racks.

"What now?" he asked, finding Ramon in the front. Ramon showed him how to turn on the dishwasher and where to store the dishes, the utensils and pots and pans.

By the end of the day Istaga had several crisp bills in his jeans pocket.

"Can you come back tomorrow?" Ramon asked.

Istaga thought for a moment and then nodded. There was something pressing against the back of his mind but the food here was good and he was hungry.

"Buy yourself a shirt before you get here tomorrow, okay?"

Istaga looked down at his bare chest, remembering where his shirt had gone. He felt a burning sensation in his upper chest as Sara's distraught face appeared in his mind. He nodded and left the café.

❧

Coyote spent the night in a shallow cave in the woods above town. But too soon he was awakened by yips and howls close by. He left his nest and hurried after them, his coyote mind driving him forward to look for something. But he didn't know what it was.

He caught up to the pack close to dawn, slinking around with his tail down to announce his lack of aggression. When the other coyotes eyed him he ducked his head, looking away. For some reason they accepted him, but whatever it was he was looking for was not there. When they ran he ran with them but when they caught a couple of rabbits and offered to share he couldn't eat. The smell of blood turned his stomach and a moment later he brought up the contents of his stomach.

He ran with the pack for many turnings of the sun but the lack of meat made him weaker and weaker until finally he couldn't go on. They whined at him, trying to get him to eat and also to come with them, but he couldn't swallow the meat and his body was not strong enough to travel that fast. He remained behind, trying not to feel the loss of their company. His human feelings were leaching over into his animal self now and it was all he could do to keep from curling up and waiting to die. When he tried to shift to Istaga nothing happened. It was Raven's appearance that finally penetrated into his addled brain.

"What's happened now?" The raven fixed him with his eye, an expression of disgust on the bird's face.

"I am looking for something."

"And what is it you are looking for?"

"I will know when I find it."

"Shift, you idiot. You'll die if you don't get something to eat. Coyotes were not meant to be vegetarians."

"I cannot shift."

"What? You can't turn into Istaga?"

"Who is Istaga?"

Raven flew to another branch watching the coyote

worriedly. This was a predicament he had not expected. "Go to the woman. She will know what to do."

"Woman?"

"Yes, the human woman who is the mother of your pup. Now go and don't look back."

"But I don't know where she is."

"Yes, you do. Stop thinking and use your instincts, if you have any left. Now go!"

Coyote limped away, his muscles so wasted that he could barely put one paw in front of the other. What had the bird told him to do? The landscape shimmered around him, going in and out of focus. He saw Toh Yah standing in the shadows beneath a tree but when he came closer the image faded away until there was nothing left. Was he on a spirit quest? Coyote wasn't aware of these sorts of things but his brain seemed oddly divided, as though there were two of him inside this animal body. Somewhere in the back of his mind was a light and in that light was a face, but Coyote didn't know whose face it was or why it was there. It was the sun hair and the sky eyes that kept him going.

18

"Sara, there's a sick coyote lying under the palo verde in the front yard."

"What?" Sara pulled the towel off her wet hair and fluffed it with her fingers, peering over Rosie's shoulder. It had been two months since her last encounter with Istaga. Nearly every day she'd hoped and prayed he would turn up at the door with their baby. "I hope that isn't Istaga."

"Whoever it is looks to be on his last legs. I've never seen a coyote that thin."

Sara carefully opened the door and headed slowly toward the animal, trying not to frighten it, but the sleeping coyote didn't even look up as she approached. Once she reached it she put a tentative hand out to touch the lank fur, her fingers feeling bone beneath the slack skin. When the animal opened its eyes she knew immediately who it was. "Istaga? Can you shift?"

The coyote closed its eyes again, letting out a low moan. Sara hurried into the house to fetch a bowl of water. "It's Istaga but he either can't or won't shift. I don't know what's wrong with him."

"Looks like he hasn't been eating. Why don't you take him a leg from the chicken we had last night?"

Sara went to the refrigerator and pulled out the Pyrex dish. She ripped a leg away from the carcass and carried it and a bowl of water out to the coyote. She placed the water by his nose and then held out the bone. "Here you go."

He opened his yellow eyes and then turned away to retch, but nothing came up.

"Rosie, he's sick! We need a vet!" she yelled.

Rosie came to join her, her worried gaze going to the prominent ribs, the dull fur. "John is the only vet I know and I'd rather not take this particular coyote to him, but I don't think we have a choice. Let's get him into the back of the truck."

ﮯﮯ

John stared down at the animal on the steel table. "He's severely dehydrated and he's starving. His teeth look fine so it's not that he can't chew. I'm giving him fluids and then we can discuss what to do with him." John gazed at Sara and Rosie, his mouth opening as he took in their expressions. "You aren't planning to keep a wild animal at your place, are you?"

"For the time being until he's well." Sara looked over at Rosie. "We happen to have a big cage from when Rosie had a puppy a while back."

"I've never seen a coyote this docile. Even the one I shot with a tranquilizer dart a few years back was wilder than this one." John looked up, his eyes meeting Sara's. "Of course that one had killed a man."

And now he's killed another man. Sara looked at Coyote, appalled by his emaciation. What had happened to him? Last time she'd seen him, that fateful day when he shifted and disappeared under the trees, he'd been magnificent, with thick shiny fur and a bushy tail. "Why won't he eat?"

"I took some blood to figure that out. But I'll tell you this--if he doesn't eat soon he'll die."

❧

By the time they got home the coyote seemed to have diminished even further, his eyes closed, his breathing shallow. They carried him to the cage in the house and placed a bowl of water next to him. "We have to do something, Rosie. Should we take him to Page to find Toh Yah?"

"Page is too far—he'll never make it."

"Do you know of another animal whisperer or healer?"

Rosie's gaze went into the distance. "I did know someone years ago. But he dealt more with humans than animals. He's part native and I swear he could heal anyone. I went to him after my husband..."

"Your husband? I didn't know you were ever married."

Rosie looked down, her expression turning sad. "It was twenty years ago now. I was nineteen. He was killed by a train."

"A train?"

Rosie nodded. "He was in his car and drunk at the time. Died instantly."

"Why didn't you ever tell me about him?"

Rosie pulled her gaze from the floor, her liquid eyes meeting Sara's. "He was the love of my life, Sara-- my soul mate. I can't bear to think about him."

"That's why you're always wanting me to forgive Istaga."

"That's right. You can't turn your back on someone who shares your destiny and your heart."

Sara stared out the window, watching the limbs of the palo verde move in the breeze. No wonder Rosie never dated. It was sad to think of this beautiful woman who had so much to give being single for the rest of her life. "Where does this guy live?"

"He used to live in a shack up in the mountains about forty miles from here. But for all I know he's dead or moved on."

"No phone I figure."

"No electronics of any kind. He thinks they mess with your head."

Sara glanced at the sleeping coyote. "Do you think he could reach the man inside this animal? The one who won't shift?"

"Istaga may have lost the ability, Sara. Just as you have."

"But why?"

"The universe has chosen to separate you two for some reason. You told me it was love that allowed you to shift that first time. Maybe you need to earn each other's love again. Just a thought."

Sara knelt next to the cage and placed her hand on Coyote's head. "I do love him," she said, her eyes filling.

"You haven't been acting like it," Rosie replied. "If you want to look for Ben we should do it soon. John said that without food this coyote isn't long for this world."

"He said he couldn't find anything physically wrong with him. But why won't he eat?"

Rosie shrugged. "Maybe he wants to die?"

"Don't say that!" Sara began to cry. "Instead of sitting here agonizing over the whys of the situation, let's get him loaded again. It's only noon. Maybe we can find Ben before it gets dark."

☙❧

Coyote was dimly aware of his surroundings. He knew he'd found the one in his mind, the one with the sun hair, but now her hair looked like the bark of the manzanita and hung to her shoulders. He didn't care much about anything anymore, his only wish to sleep and never wake up. And he was pretty sure that would happen soon.

There was a shiver of a memory of when he could change his shape and hold the woman in his arms, but it only brought more pain. He could tell that the woman was very upset, could hear it in the high-pitched way she spoke and how her hand gently stroked his fur. When they picked him up again and carried him out to the truck he wondered where they were taking him. Maybe they would leave him in the desert so that when he died other animals could feed on him. For a moment he had an odd sensation — something inside that didn't want to end things — something that knew he could have this woman again if he could only...what? And then his eyes closed and he fell into a place of darkness.

"Hang on," he heard Raven caw. "Keep breathing in and out, in and out. You must have the will to live, Coyote. This woman loves you and you love her. Remember that. I know where they are taking you and this man will help you. Just hang on."

Coyote tried to focus on the enormous raven but the bird's image seemed to fade in and out, and then he was falling, falling into a pit so deep he never thought he would reach the bottom.

❧

Sara pulled open the window between the truck bed and the cab, terror making her voice shrill. "Hurry, Rosie! He's unconscious!" Sara had the coyote's head in her lap and was monitoring his breathing, which seemed to stop and start in fits.

"We're almost there!" Rosie called back. "Now just pray Ben is there!"

The truck bumped and swayed up the rutted dirt road, the engine straining. Deep forest stood silent on both sides of the narrow track, the only sounds were the tires slipping and catching as they crept higher and higher. When Sara tried to see ahead it was as though a haze had appeared, obliterating the view. It was creepy and if she'd been driving she would have turned the truck around and driven out of here as fast as she could. "Are you sure this is the right way?" she yelled.

"Ben hides where he lives, Sara—that's the reason for the fog!"

"He's a sorcerer?" Sara called out.

"I guess you could call him that, but that word

makes me think of someone who dabbles in the dark arts. Ben is full of light."

A minute later the fog lifted, revealing a driveway on the right. A sign hung crookedly from two posts. Come only in peace.

"This is it!" Rosie yelled, turning off and heading up a road lined with grass and wildflowers. Here the trees were less densely packed, with hardwoods and dogwood mixed in with the pines, cedars and spruce. Sunlight slanted through, turning everything golden. Sara was transfixed by the fairytale scene opening up on both sides of the truck—butterflies of every hue fluttered by, birds called, their sweet trills echoing through the forest. There was an aura of serenity here. "This doesn't look like the desert!" she yelled through the open window.

Rosie slowed the truck and turned to look back. "Ben's here. If he wasn't it wouldn't feel like this."

A few seconds later a small log house came into view, smoke drifting lazily from a stone chimney. A couple of rabbits were grazing on the grass close to the cabin and Sara was pretty sure she saw a deer or two under the trees that surrounded the house. Birdsong filled her ears, the trills and varied calls indicating many species.

Rosie climbed out of the truck at the same time a man of indeterminate age appeared on the porch, shading his eyes to get a look. Brown wavy hair threaded with gray hung around his square face. He wore a heavy plaid shirt, jeans and work boots. He was not what Sara had expected. When he saw Rosie he broke into a wide smile, striding toward her.

A second later he lifted her into the air and swung her around. Once she was on the ground again he turned to Sara, his gray eyes quizzical. "I sense something here," he said. "You are not what you seem."

Rosie grabbed his arm. "Ben, we brought you a very sick coyote. I hope you can help him."

Ben moved to the truck and climbed into the bed. He bent over Coyote and sniffed him before lifting him in his arms. Sara lowered the back so that he could get out easier and then Rosie and Sara followed him up the couple of steps to the porch and into the house.

"He is also not what he seems," Ben muttered, placing the coyote in front of the fire where several logs crackled and spit. The large man kneeled in front of the coyote, turning his kind gray eyes on Sara. "What has happened to this animal?"

Sara glanced toward Rosie who nodded to let her know it was okay to be honest with this man. "He's a shifter, was granted this ability by a man who called himself a shaman. We fell in love and had a baby. But now he can't shift and I can't change into a coyote."

He looked up from where he was examining the coyote. "So you were also given this gift?"

Sara shook her head. "I don't know how it happened. But suddenly I could do it. I always maintained it was love."

Ben nodded, turning back to his patient. "This coyote is starving. Why is that?"

"He refuses to eat," Sara answered.

"Tell me everything that has happened to him in the last few months."

"I...I haven't seen him for two months, but before that I..." Sara hesitated wondering how much she wanted to reveal.

"Before that this coyote saved Sara from four men who were about to rape her," Rosie finished. "And Sara was upset because this coyote killed one of them."

Ben frowned and glanced at Sara before moving his attention back to the coyote on the rug. "Did you have a conversation with his human side?"

Sara nodded, not wanting to revisit that horrible day. "I told him it was his fault that our baby shifted and took off with a coyote pack and I accused him of being a murderer."

Ben didn't change expression when these words came out of her mouth but Sara was now crying, tears tracking down her face and dripping onto the floor. All of this was her fault.

Ben placed a hand on the coyote's head and closed his eyes. A few moments later he said, "This animal will no longer eat meat and this is why he is dying. He must have associated the killing and your accusations with the smell of blood. As to not being able to shift, I don't know what is preventing it—but if he cannot shift to his human form we will not save him. Coyotes supplement their diet with berries and seeds and so on, but ultimately if they don't get some meat they won't survive."

Sara felt a sharp pain in her chest. "What can we do?"

At that moment there was a loud cawing outside. Ben pushed himself up. "Raven is here to help," he said, moving quickly toward the door. When he flung it open an enormous raven flew in, it's dark, almost menacing eye going to the coyote lying in front of the fire. The bird made a sound that grated against Sara's nerves—like chalk on a blackboard. Ben seemed to be in communication with the raven, nodding as the bird made several more sharp sounds.

"What is he saying?" Sara asked.

"He is very familiar with Coyote-man, the name he calls him. He says the man is trapped inside the coyote and can't get out without a ceremony."

"What kind of ceremony?" Rosie asked.

"I will let the bird help me decide. But now I have to fetch my drum and my feathers and the bowl to hold his soul."

Ben left the room and Sara could hear him rummaging around, the crash of something falling to the floor and then a string of curse words. " I thought he was a holy man," she whispered.

Rosie chuckled. "He's an earthy holy man," Rosie whispered back.

Sara glanced at the bird sitting on a rafter above them. She almost expected it to start talking. Letting her gaze go from the ceiling to the room she noticed the strange artifacts that filled the space. Stacks of small stones like tiny cairns had been placed on the wide windowsills, as well as bits of bone. A Native American flute was displayed on hooks in the wall and a hand woven rug hung next to it. There was no real furniture, only cushions and a window seat that was covered in more cushions. In a nook to one side she spied a sort of kitchen with a sink and a very small stove with cabinets above it. Bunches of herbs and some dried flowers hung from the rafters. She could smell their pungent aroma as she stared upward. The house was tiny and yet it felt spacious, almost as though there was more room than she could see with her mortal eyes.

A moment later Ben reappeared with a stick of sage, a drum, a rattle, a copper bowl, and a group of golden brown feathers that looked as though they'd been sewn together to make a fan. He placed the rattle, the bowl, the drum and the feathers down next to Coyote and stuck the sage into the fire to light it. Once it was burning he began to chant, moving the sage stick around the coyote and using his hand to wave the smoke in Coyote's direction.

Sara's eyes began to water as the room filled with the pungent aroma. When she looked up she couldn't see the raven but she could still hear his bill clacking as he rubbed it along the rafter. A drum began to beat, reminding her of Toh Yah and the sweat lodge she'd participated in three years before. The sweat and her spirit animal, (the hawk) had instructed her about whether or not to give herself over to Coyote and Istaga. That moment had settled something deep inside her, allowing her access to what lay in her heart. And here again the sound moved through her body, delving into that same place inside her. She glanced at Rosie who had her eyes closed and was chanting.

Ben startled her when he handed her the rattle.

"Shake," he told her.

The rhythmic sound of the rattle, the drum beat and the chanting had a hypnotic effect and Sara found herself drifting in a place that seemed not here. She was a coyote and then a human, she and Istaga were making love on the floor of a cave and a moment later they were coupling as coyotes. Istaga was helping her through the birth of their child--she was crying out in pain and then a second later she was lying still with the newborn in her arms. Istaga was crying, his tears landing on her bare skin as he kissed her and their child, welcoming Kaliska into the world. They were traveling, first as coyotes and then shifting into their human forms, cooking food over the fire, loving each other, laughing, sleeping, hunting as coyotes, all of it muddled into scenes that flew by. Her heart felt like it would burst with happiness when she saw their baby's first steps, the smile on Kaliska's face as she held out her arms to be picked up. Istaga was there for all of it, his presence making her feel safe and loved.

"I command your human soul to come to us!" Ben shouted, scaring Sara so much that she almost dropped the rattle. "I command you to be your full self, every part of yourself!" he bellowed.

The drum was louder now, the beat coming faster. Sara felt a whirring in her ears as though something or someone was entering the house. She cringed in anticipation of whatever it might be. She heard the raven caw several times and then heard his wings beating as he flew in swooping circles above them. Rosie was still chanting, the words mingling with the drum and the rattle and whatever energy had been summoned. And then as suddenly as it began there was utter silence and the rattle dropped from her hand. Through the gloom of smoke she saw Istaga curled up on the floor, his chest bare, ribs sticking out like a famine victim.

Sara let out a cry and then sobbed, her fingers smoothing the tangled hair back from the pale skin of his forehead. He was horribly thin, his cheekbones jutting, his chest sunken. His eyes were closed, lashes dark against the hollows beneath them. When she glanced toward Ben his focus was on the bowl. He was burning something there, something that smelled of light and sun and meadow wildflowers. The raven landed next to Istaga and clacked his bill several times before flying straight through the open door and away.

Istaga opened his eyes and looked at Sara. He reached out to take her hand and then clasped it against his chest. "I thought I..." his voice caught and he couldn't go on, tears tracking down his cheeks as his yellow eyes met hers.

"I'm sorry, I'm so sorry," Sara whispered, leaning against him. "I love you so much."

Istaga sighed and then closed his eyes and this time his breathing was normal.

"Let him rest. When he wakes he can eat."

"But no meat?"

Ben smiled, revealing straight white teeth. "I'll fix him a vegetarian meal," he said.

❦

The meal they had was a delicious stew of root vegetables served with home baked bread and thick slices of sharp cheddar. Ben had brought out a flannel shirt for Istaga that was way too big for him and they'd propped him up on pillows since he was too weak to sit. Sara spooned stew into his mouth, wiping his mouth with a napkin when it dripped. He ate some cheese on his own but he was full before half the food was gone.

There wasn't a lot of conversation, all of them seeming in awe about what had just happened, Sara in particular. She couldn't believe what Ben had managed and kept thinking about the chanting, the bird and the drums, as though they were dream images. When she glanced down she saw the drum, the rattle and the bowl, but the feathers were gone and she wondered what their purpose had been.

It was dark by the time Ben gathered up the bowls and plates and carried them to the sink. Rosie got off the floor and followed him, their mumbled conversation impossible to make out. It didn't matter since Sara was now lying close to Istaga who had already fallen asleep. Sara fell asleep with her head on his chest, his arm wrapped tight around her.

❦

When Sara woke the sky was pale gray and the birds were just waking up. She heard conversation coming from the other room and realized that Rosie had spent the night with Ben. Whether anything besides friendship was happening between them she didn't know. Istaga was still asleep, some of his pallor gone. But she knew his recovery would be slow. She lay back, resting her hand on Istaga's thigh just to make sure he was really there.

"Sara," she heard him say and turned to see him gazing at her.

Somehow he had the strength to wrap his arm around her and pull her toward him, his mouth meeting hers in a kiss. But it was only a second before he fell back, his eyes closing in exhaustion.

"Are you all right?" she whispered.

"Not strong enough for the feelings that just came over me." He smiled weakly. "I want you badly, but…"

Sara glanced at the closed door. "We couldn't even if you could," she said, placing a hand on his cheek.

Istaga chuckled. "Can you fix me something to eat? I'm starving."

Sara went to the little alcove to search for food but before she came up with anything Ben appeared from the bedroom wearing only jeans. "Bread and eggs," he said, heading to the front door.

"Where is he going?" Sara asked Rosie who appeared in the bedroom doorway.

"Chickens," Rosie answered, running her fingers through her tangled curls. She was wearing one of Ben's enormous denim shirts, her eyes at half-mast. "Coffee?" she asked.

"I don't know where he keeps it."

Rosie entered the alcove and searched through cupboards, coming up with a small paper bag. She seemed familiar with the set-up as she found a jug of water and poured it into a pan, placing it on a burner. A second later the flame was going and Rosie was spooning coffee into the water. "Cowboy coffee," she announced, turning to smile at Sara. "How is the patient this morning?"

"He's better but still really weak. It's going to take a while."

"At least I'm alive," Istaga muttered with his eyes closed.

Sara laughed. "And hungry, which is the best part."

"Not the best," Istaga said, opening his eyes to gaze on Sara.

Once the coffee was hot Rosie poured it into two cups, handing one to Sara. "Does Istaga drink coffee?"

Sara shook her head.

Ben arrived with a basket full of eggs and proceeded to cook them up with some herbs he pulled from the rafters. He sliced bread and passed plates around as though having three people in his house was a common occurrence. But Sara knew he lived alone and had few visitors. She could tell that the chatter of conversation going on between Sara and Rosie was distracting for him.

When breakfast was over Rosie put her hand on Ben's arm. "Why don't you take a walk while I clean up? We'll be ready to go by the time you get back."

The larger than life man who had just brought about a miracle gazed at her with an expression of confusion. "Rosie, I…"

"It's all right, Ben. Now go."

After Ben left the house Sara helped Rosie pick up the plates and watched her friend find the soap and begin to clean them. She rinsed each one, handing them to Sara to dry and stack on the counter. "What's going on with you two?" Sara asked.

"Ben and me?" Rosie smiled wistfully. "We've known each other for twenty years."

Sara smirked. "There's more to it than that. I see the way he looks at you. And you spent the night together."

Rosie laughed. "Yes, we care for each other, but how can I have a relationship with a man who lives in the back of beyond? We realized years ago that it wouldn't work."

Sara scoffed. "And I'm in love with a coyote. How much more difficult could it be?"

When Rosie turned her eyes were filled with tears. "Please don't talk about it anymore," she begged, wiping her eyes with the dishtowel she took out of Sara's hand.

By the time Ben got back to the house Rosie had dressed and arranged things in the truck for the ride home. Sara had not brought up Ben again, instead helping Istaga out of the house so he could pee in the bushes.

When they were getting ready to leave Istaga unbuttoned the shirt and was in the process of taking it off when Ben said, "Keep the damn shirt, Coyote-man. You need it more than I do."

"Thank you for bringing me back," Istaga said. "I

know I would have died if it had not been for what you did."

Ben smiled and clasped Istaga's forearm in a gesture of friendship before turning to say goodbye to Rosie. "Come anytime," he said, reaching out and pulling her close. "I'm always here for you." When they pulled apart they both had tears in their eyes.

Ben turned to Sara, his gray eyes moving from her to Istaga. "Take good care of each other."

Sara smiled up at him and then settled her gaze on Istaga standing next to her, his hand on her shoulder for support. "We will," she answered. "And thank you for everything."

Rosie climbed behind the wheel and turned the key and the truck roared to life. Sara climbed in next to her and then reached over to help Istaga. They all waved as Rosie headed down the driveway and into the fog.

19

$\mathcal{T}$hree weeks had gone by since the trip into the mountains to the man Sara now referred to as the miracle worker. Istaga grew stronger every day. Sara left him in Rosie's house every weekday and Saturday mornings to go to her job at the café in San Manuel. Without that money she would have nothing to contribute to the living situation that Rosie was providing them.

Sara was late for work and drove fast, her mind on Istaga. He was still not strong enough to make love, which was a good thing since she didn't feel ready to take that step. They slept curled together as they had in the past but there was something that kept Sara apart—something inside her that she couldn't get hold of. So far they had not spoken about Kaliska and what to do about finding her. Sara was afraid to bring it up, worried that it might lead to another argument, which was the last thing she wanted right now. They were just beginning to trust one another and until he was back to himself she wanted to keep the conversation as light as possible. He had not spoken about shifting and as far as she knew hadn't shifted since that fateful day when Ben had brought the man part of him back from wherever it had gone.

The memories of the past plagued her, especially

when she was away from him, on the road like this morning. How would they ever get beyond the death of that man and their baby being gone? Surely the authorities had learned of the two deaths by now. And if she knew him at all, Raleigh had gotten wind of it and was hot on Istaga's trail.

"You're late!" Joe yelled when she parked the truck. "Why can't you get here on time?" He stood with hands on hips glaring at her.

"I'm sorry, Joe. Istaga is still very weak and needs my help. He can barely get to the bathroom without me."

Joe's belligerent stare softened. "It must be hard for you with an invalid to take care of. What about your daughter?"

Sara followed him into the kitchen, noticing several customers in the front. "Nothing so far, and I don't want to bring it up to Istaga until he's stronger."

Joe nodded. "What do the police say?"

Sara tried to come up with a suitable lie. "They have no leads," she finally answered, carrying the plates he dished out into the front room.

❧

Istaga worked his way outside and let his water go. He could get along without a cane now and the food Rosie prepared and left for him was satisfying and filling. When he came back inside he opened the refrigerator and pulled out the plate of bean enchiladas, spooning it into his mouth with his fingers. He liked the heat and spice she cooked with.

He scanned the walls that surrounded him, and felt them closing in. He felt a need to move, to run, but his body was not up to it. He longed for freedom, the sensation of running across fields on four legs. This life was getting duller by the day. The only thing he looked forward to was lying next to Sara at night, but even that was frustrating now with his inability to mate. How long would it be until he was strong enough?

Sara hadn't yet spoken about Kaliska but he knew she thought about her all the time—he could see the sadness in her sky eyes. If and when she brought it up would be a difficult day, he thought, his gaze going outside where the wind blew through the bare limbs of the tree in the front yard, making them sway. The hot time was over and days were short. Soon the white rain would come in the mountains. He wondered where Kaliska was right now. Had she found a mate? Would she have pups in the spring? If it was up to him he'd let her have her life. Once a pup was full-grown they often moved on. He didn't have any misgivings about it. But humans were different, and he knew that Sara could not give her up.

He shook his head in frustration and slumped onto the couch. He had to mate with Sara soon—feeling her body next to his every night and not being able to do the one thing that linked them was making him loco. If she had another pup would she stop obsessing over Kaliska? If only he could make her understand— Kaliska was gone.

When Sara entered the house around five thirty Istaga was sound asleep on the couch. His head was turned away, his long hair hanging across his face. He was filling out again, his cheeks not so drawn, his chest muscular. A shock of attraction moved through her, leaving her breathless for a second.

Istaga woke when she placed her hand on his cheek, his yellow gaze meeting hers. "Sara," he said, catching her hand and pulling her down next to him.

She let him kiss her, knowing that this was as far as things could go until he recovered, but this time he didn't stop, his hands roaming across her body like a starving animal. "Sara," he moaned.

Before she had fully comprehended what was happening Istaga had managed to remove the clothing that needed to be removed and was on top of her, his hands in her hair. "Istaga, no," she said, trying to push him off.

He stared at her in confusion. "Why?"

"I'm not ready," she told him, but she *was* ready and her body was screaming at her to shut up.

Istaga waited, propped on his elbows. "I can do this, if that's what you're worried about."

"It's not that...I..."

"You told me you love me."

"I do love you."

Istaga rolled off and sat on the edge of the couch with his head in his hands. "I do not understand."

Sara pulled on her underwear and tugged her skirt

down over her hips. "We need to talk first, Istaga. I have things on my mind."

"Talk before this?"

Sara nodded, her gaze going to the window. "Rosie's home. Put your jeans on."

Istaga picked his jeans up off the floor and headed to the bedroom, closing the door behind him.

When Rosie walked through the door Sara was sitting on the couch as though nothing had happened. "Hey. How was your day?"

Rosie took one look at her and made a face. "What's going on here? You look guilty, or ashamed, or something. What happened?" Rosie scanned the room. "Where's Istaga?"

"He's in the bedroom."

Rosie went to the refrigerator and pulled out a couple of beers. "Are you going to share or do I have to beat it out of you?"

Sara took the bottle Rosie handed her and twisted off the cap. "It's nothing," she said, taking a hefty swig.

Rosie let out a sigh. "If you say so."

৵৵

When Istaga did not emerge for dinner Sara went to check on him. But when she opened the bedroom door the window was wide open and Istaga was gone.

Rosie peeked into the room. "Where is he?"

Sara tried to wipe the tears from her eyes before Rosie saw them but she was too late.

"Sara! What did you do?"

"Why is it always me?" Sara whined, sitting on the

edge of the bed. "All I did was tell him we needed to talk before we made love—what's wrong with that?"

"Apparently he didn't agree with you," Rosie said, crossing the room to close the window. "Now tell me what happened."

After Sara relayed the scene on the couch Rosie shook her head. "You are seriously the most stubborn woman I've ever known. The man needed to prove to you he was whole again and you brushed him off? Now he's out there with no money, no way to eat and no place to stay. And if he shifts he'll be in a worse predicament."

Sara stared at her friend. "I wasn't ready, Rosie! I haven't sorted through everything yet!"

"For once in your life couldn't you have given in?"

"And what about you?" Sara asked angrily. "You and Ben love each other and here you are down here while he stays up there. Is this stupid job of yours so important that it keeps you from the one thing in life that's important?"

"And who's talking about love? What you just did to that man is beyond my understanding, Sara! He nearly died and you're quibbling about needing to talk? He's a coyote and thinks in terms of the physical. Talking is a completely alien concept. You of all people should understand that!" Rosie turned and left the room.

Sara heard her in the kitchen, banging pots and pans around. She and Rosie had never argued like this. She sat on the bed and tried to think, but all she could do was cry. Rosie was right. Connecting physically would have made them both feel better and probably opened the way for talking, but instead she'd driven him away. What in the world was wrong with her? And where had he gone?

20

*I*staga stumbled down the road away from Black Base and Sara. His thoughts were jumbled and he couldn't make sense of what had happened—he only knew that he couldn't stay there any longer. Sara said she loved him, a word that seemed to mean she wanted to be with him always, but he knew it wasn't true. She did not behave as she had before the killing on the mountain and Kaliska's disappearance.

He had waited to be strong enough, and today it had happened. But she pushed him away, saying she needed to talk. What was there to talk about? He frowned and then let out a sob that lifted into the sky above him. He had to forget her and find another mate.

He looked up when someone honked, a truck narrowly missing him as he ran across the road. Once he reached the weeds on the other side he tested his ability to shift and found that he could still do it. Good, because his human side was aching all over and felt heavy, his eyes leaking water as never before.

❦

Coyote headed in a certain direction, not knowing exactly why. He slept under a mesquite tree and in the morning he was off again, following a route he didn't understand. It was cold and he was glad of his fur. But as he began to climb into the mountains he had to rest more often, his strength ebbing from lack of food. When he finally reached the road that led up to the ridge he was moving at a walk and wasn't sure he could make it. But when he reached the place of fog and mists he had a sudden surge of energy. Why was he here? But his coyote brain didn't work that way. It was instinct that had brought him this far. When he picked up the sweet scent of flowers and freshly cut grass his body relaxed. He was nearly there.

"Where did you come from?"

Coyote heard the familiar voice, opening his eyes to look up at the man standing over him. He was too tired to stay awake and put his head back down on his front paws. He felt the man's arms come under his body and didn't struggle as he was carried inside.

"What has happened?" the man asked once Coyote was on the rug in front of the fire. "Have you lost the human part of you again? Shift, I need to talk to Istaga."

The words were a command and coyote understood. Sara had said this word many times. He did as the man asked, his underdressed body shivering from the cold wind that blew from the open door.

The man moved to the door and closed it before addressing him. "Istaga, tell me why you are here?"

Istaga sat up and pulled the shirt around his body. "I had nowhere else to go."

"What about Sara and Rosie? Weren't you staying with them?"

"Sara does not want me."

Ben sat on the floor next to him. "When she was here I only saw her love for you."

Istaga shook his head. "She will not mate with me."

A smile quirked at the corners of Ben's mouth. "Did she say she needed to talk first?"

"How did you know?"

"It is often the way with human women. Talking is their way of making sense of things. Men are more apt to forget the talking and do the deed."

Istaga nodded. "It wasn't only that. I couldn't stay in that house with nothing to do. I had to get out. I know Sara is angry with me about our pup and she is also angry about the man I killed."

"Istaga, you were protecting her. If you hadn't killed him there is a good chance Sara would be dead right now."

"I know that but she does not. She will not listen to me."

Ben looked away. "I'm not sure what you expect me to do."

"Something drew me here. I can no longer run with the pack."

Ben's wide face creased into a smile. "A vegetarian coyote is an oxymoron."

Istaga frowned. "An oxy-what?"

"It's a word that means it's contradictory. A coyote not eating meat doesn't make sense."

"Will I get over this?"

"I don't know, Istaga—will you?"

Istaga shook his head. "I tried on the way here but it had the same effect as before. My stomach refuses it.

Can you help me with this?"

"Help you get over your aversion to meat? I don't know. I've never done any work like that. Are you sure that's the problem you want me to solve?"

Istaga felt confused, his gaze meeting Ben's. "Is there another?"

Ben chuckled. "You are in love with a human woman who, despite your worry, loves you too. You have a child together who is missing. If you found your pup do you think that might help Sara get over her anger?"

Istaga stared into the distance. "If I found Kaliska Sara would be very happy."

"And would she mate with you then?"

Istaga smiled. "Yes."

"Well then, that is your task. You must find your child and bring her back to her mother."

Istaga felt the water start and tried to wipe it away. "Kaliska has found a mate and runs with a pack. How can I find her? And if I did find her how could I convince her to leave her mate? Coyotes mate for life."

"There is a chance she has not yet found a mate."

"Where do I start? I have no idea where to look."

Ben pushed himself up and went into the other room. When he came back he had the sage stick and the copper bowl. "Are you willing to do a finding ceremony?"

It was nighttime and Coyote was in a realm he didn't recognize, filled with enormous trees that seemed to watch him. Raven sat on a branch of one of these, insisting that Coyote follow the bird's orders. "You will remain here while I fly ahead and scout. If I find the pack she's with I will come back and get you."

Coyote shivered, looking up at the cold stars that filled the black dome above him. This had to work. He heard a drumbeat and then another and then the swish of feathers as Raven lifted, blending into the black night and disappearing. A familiar voice said words Coyote did not understand and then the drum began again. The sound was hypnotic and he drifted in the moments of silence between the beats. The smell of burning sage filled his nostrils and he wondered if there was a fire in the underbrush. But he saw no smoke, no sign of it in the solemn trees that lined the hollow where he waited. He heard the caw as Raven flew over him, the bird landing next to him on noisy wings.

"She is just over the next ridge," Raven announced. "Follow me."

Istaga opened his eyes, surprised to find himself still in front of the fire in Ben's cabin. "I thought I was…"

Ben nodded and put a hand on his shoulder. "The raven is here and will lead you." He pointed toward the bird sitting above them on a rafter. "But first you must fill your belly so that coyote will have the strength to travel. Kaliska is far from here. When you reach her you must shift into Istaga and convince her to shift with you. If she refuses you cannot take her away from the pack."

Ben got up and headed into the other room, coming back with a large bowl of stew. "This will sustain you for a day or two, but do not tarry."

After eating every bit of the stew Istaga and the

raven left the cabin. It was dusk and he knew there would no sleep tonight and maybe none the next night either. Raven flew ahead, leading up the road away from Ben's cabin. The air was thin and Istaga could feel the strain on his lungs, his muscles growing tired more quickly than normal. But then again he was still recovering.

Once they reached the top of the ridge he had a view of the ranges that led south into Mexico. They piled one on top of the other, spreading into the hazy distance like a mirage. When the bird landed by him a moment later and let out a series of calls, he understood. He had to travel as Coyote or he would never make it.

The raven and the coyote reached the river early the next morning and followed it south. Raven flew ahead again while Coyote stopped to drink and rest for a few minutes. He was exhausted and his pads were sore from the sharp rocks he'd been traveling over.

His mind was lost in a blur of imagery that he couldn't decipher. He saw a coyote pup, his, and then a human baby girl. He tried to understand what this meant but his fuzzy coyote brain was not up to the task. When Raven returned he tried to communicate his confusion but the bird ignored him, gathering nuts in his beak and dropping them.

Something about the nuts caused Coyote to shift into Istaga, his stomach rumbling at the idea of food. He picked up the broken shell scooping out the nutmeat and popping it into his mouth. He looked up at Raven who dropped another nut and then another, their shells cracking as they landed on the rocks.

By the time Istaga shifted into Coyote he was feeling better, his stomach at least partially filled. Raven shook out his feathers and took off over the tops of the trees leaving Coyote to follow along the river.

It was nighttime again before Raven gave a sign that he'd spotted the pack, the bird fluttering up and down with excitement. Coyote followed him away from the river and up a steep hill, down into a valley on the other side and then up another hill. On the far side Coyote could hear the yips and howls from the pack. He listened carefully before he recognized Kaliska's voice.

"What do I do now?" he asked once he'd shifted into human form. "They will run if they see me or smell me."

Raven looked down from where he perched on a pine branch, his dark eyes pinning him with their intensity. Istaga locked eyes with the bird until he received the message. He had to stay Coyote until he found Kaliska and separated her from the rest of them. If he couldn't do that he would fail.

Once he'd shifted they set out, keeping a safe distance from the hunting pack. Coyote heard his pup in the midst and let out a howl before he realized what he was doing. The wary coyotes came close and circled around him, eyeing the stranger. What did he want? Where had he come from? One of them attacked him but then a smaller female ran up and managed to stop the older male. Coyote and the female sniffed noses and then circled each other. This was his pup.

Now what was he supposed to do? The other coyotes went back to what they were doing, leaving the younger female behind. He could hear their yips and calls growing fainter. Once they were out of sight Raven flew down and began to caw loudly, urging Coyote to do something. But what was it? Raven flew at him, pecking and attacking until finally Coyote got the message. When he shifted the small coyote next to him cringed in fear, her eyes wide and scared.

"Kaliska, it's me. Don't you remember? Shift Kaliska."

The coyote stared at him with eyes the same shade as Sara's. Istaga felt the water start and wiped his eyes. "Please, little one. You have to shift. I need you, your mother needs you."

Raven cawed a warning as the coyotes began to circle back for the female. Istaga reached out with both hands, grabbed his pup and ran.

The coyote wriggled and yipped and then bit him on the arm, drawing blood. But he didn't let go. He finally stopped when he could no longer hear the rest of the pack. "Kaliska, you have to shift. You know how." But the coyote didn't shift and seemed more afraid than she had been at first.

"I'll have to tie you up," Istaga told her. "I can't get any rest knowing you'll take off. Don't you remember me or your mother?"

Kaliska eyed him warily, her tail between her legs. Istaga let out a sigh and took off his shirt and tore it into strips. He tied one piece around her neck and attached the other end to his belt. "At least I can sleep for a moment or two," he told her, closing his eyes.

Istaga woke when he felt a tug on the end of the strip of cloth. And then he heard a gurgle and a baby voice said, "Da."

He picked up his baby girl and hugged her close, surprised by how much she'd grown. Her hair was long and curly, her face round and plump. Her little legs were sturdy now and when she walked it wasn't the toddling unsteady gait he remembered. "Your mother is waiting for us, Kaliska. We have to travel as quickly as we can."

Istaga formed a sort of papoose out of limbs he pulled off the conifers and tied Kaliska into it with the shirt strips. He made straps with the sleeves and then slung the contraption onto his back. Raven led the way up and down the many hills they'd crossed, stopping at intervals so that Kaliska and Istaga could drink water and rest.

Sometime during the cold day the baby began to cry and kept crying for several hours. He knew she was hungry but he couldn't risk having her shift. It was Raven that came to their rescue, discovering a stream filled with watercress and some bushes that had a few dried berries still left on them. It wasn't much but it quieted her and this time when they took off she fell asleep on his back.

By that night Istaga was cold, hungry and exhausted, but he couldn't risk stopping. The baby had nothing to wear, nothing to eat—he had to get back to the house as fast as possible. Traveling on two legs was slow going compared to four and he began to doubt his decision to make this trip. But Raven kept encouraging him on with his swooping and cawing, trying to keep him from giving up. By now Kaliska was shivering with cold, her little moans of hunger worrying him. When he finally stopped to rest again her lips were blue, her face mottled and red. "We need to shift," he told her. "It's the only way we can stay warm." This time she obeyed.

They spent some time in a small cave he found, their fur keeping them warm and toasty. When they woke again the world outside was white and flakes were still falling. Coyote nosed his pup, urging her to hunt with him. They'd done it many times before and Kaliska was happy to oblige. She caught a rabbit before he did and devoured it so quickly that he could barely register his own nausea. She offered to share but he declined, turning his head away in disgust. She seemed content after that, running next to him and following the raven. Traveling as coyotes took them half the time and before he knew it they had come down into the valley and were close to Black Base.

Just before they arrived in town he shifted and coaxed Kaliska to shift as well. They didn't have far to go now. He had the baby in his arms and was crossing the main street when a red truck slowed down and a familiar face peered out the window. Before he could think what to do the man was out the door and had clamped a hand firmly down on his shoulder. "Time for you to be put away for good," Raleigh said, grabbing the baby out of his arms. "If you do what I say I'll let her live."

Kaliska shifted and pulled out of his arms, racing for the field next to the road and flaming the fires of Raleigh's outrage.

Raleigh pointed the gun at Istaga's chest. "Mark my words. You and your beast child and the sick and depraved woman you live with will end your lives behind bars. Now take me to Sara and I won't kill you right now."

Istaga hadn't thought twice about what to do next, his instinct only to disarm the man and get away. When he shifted, Raleigh's gun went off, the bullet missing him by inches. And then he'd attacked, his jaws clamping onto Raleigh's shoulder as the man twisted to get away He was just going for the throat when he heard the police sirens.

21

$\mathcal{S}$ara was driving home from work when she saw a dark-haired man next to the road holding a baby in his arms. She slowed down to get a better look. At the same time a red truck came from the other direction and stopped next to him. When Sara saw Raleigh jump out of the truck and grab Istaga by the shoulder she pulled off the road, ready to do battle, rage clenching her belly.

She hopped out of Rosie's truck and hurried toward them but before she got there Kaliska had shifted and wriggled out of Istaga's arms. A second later the coyote was racing across the empty lot next to the road, dodging cat's claw acacia and prickly pears. Sara crossed the road at a run and took off after her.

It was only when she had crossed the field and climbed the fence on the other side and headed into the wild desert beyond that she realized she was coyote. Her mind was not as quick in this form and her thoughts were tangled and confused by what she was doing. She could see the younger female in the distance and knew there was some reason she needed to reach her, but why was a question she couldn't answer.

The younger coyote was frightened and seemed confused, running erratically. It wasn't difficult to catch up with her. Sara shifted without thinking about it when she saw the coyote hiding under a hackberry bush. "Kaliska, it's me, you mother," she said soothingly, approaching the coyote slowly. The coyote's eyes were wide with fear, her tail pinned between her hind legs. "Shift, sweet one."

But the coyote didn't shift and in the next moment the animal hurtled out of her hiding place and took off again. When Sara tried to shift nothing happened. She collapsed on the ground, watching the coyote disappear into the heavy brush on the other side of the field. There was no way a human could crawl through that mass of prickly bushes.

It was a few minutes later that she heard sirens in the distance and scanned back toward the road. The red truck was still there but now there were several police cars pulled over next to it. Either Istaga had killed the bastard or Raleigh had called the cops on him. Neither scenario sounded good.

She heard the ambulance coming from a distance and watched it pull up in back of all the other cars. A moment later she noticed a coyote running her way. For a second she thought it was Kaliska, but then realized how large it was. When he reached her Istaga shifted, his face red, his breath coming in gasps.

"We have to get out of here," he said, turning to look back. "They saw where I went. Where is Kaliska?"

"She headed that way," Sara answered, pointing. "What happened back there?"

"You do not want to know." Istaga shifted, his yellow-eyed gaze watching her. Down the hill she saw several uniformed men climbing over the fence with their guns drawn. When Coyote turned and loped away Sara ran after him, her only thought to keep him from danger and find their baby. The adrenaline and fear for their lives must have allowed her to shift because soon she was running on four legs. The two of them slipped under the brush and headed toward the mountains, following Kaliska's scent.

Sara as a coyote knew they had to keep running. There was something back there, something dangerous. She kept up with the large male coyote in front of her— her mate. They ran until they came into the mountains, the male stopping first. She put her nose in the air searching for their pup but did not pick up her scent. And then they were both on two legs, facing each other in a wilderness of mesquite and cactus.

"I don't know where she went," Sara said, watching Istaga. She felt dizzy and disoriented, as though she'd arrived in a completely different world. What were they doing and why were they here?

"How did you shift?" Istaga asked.

Sara shook her head. "I think it happened because of Kaliska. I was trying to catch her."

"But you did it again with me."

"We were chasing Kaliska, or so I thought. Did you kill him?"

Istaga shook his head. "No. The police arrived and I had to get out of there."

Sara stared into the distance. "I have to say I wouldn't have minded if you did. As long as he's alive that man will never leave us alone."

"So now you approve of me killing someone? Make

up your mind."

Sara heard the anger and frustration behind his words, turning to face him again. "I'm sorry, Istaga. I'm sorry for everything. All I care about now is finding my baby and keeping her with me."

"In her human form?" Istaga's eyes narrowed and turned dark.

"Of course in human form. What good would it do me to keep a coyote?"

"We could form a pack, Sara. We could be together as a family, live the way we used to live."

Sara shook her head, her eyes filling. "It will never work. If being a coyote is more important than your love for me then I guess we should say goodbye now."

"When we were first together, you…"

"Too much has happened since then," she interrupted. "And it isn't enough for me. I found that out when we were up in those mountains for months on end. I'm a human and I have human needs. I like good food and conversation and watching movies. I want to get my computer business going." When she looked at Istaga he was staring at the ground with a frown on his face. "And what about you?" she continued. "Being a vegetarian coyote doesn't work."

Istaga looked up. "I hope to get over that."

"And if you don't?"

He sighed and ran his fingers through his long hair, pulling out the tangles. "Sara, I can't live in an enclosed space. I need to run and to feel the wind in my fur, smell the pinesap and sage and hear the call of my own kind. When it is silent my heart sings—the noise of a city drowns out what I need to hear. "

"Then I guess we should part ways now. It'll be harder if we spend time together." Sara held his gaze, noticing the tears welling in his eyes.

"What about our pup?" he asked. "Are you giving up?"

"Can you track her? Because I can't."

"She hasn't gone far. She's not familiar with this area so she's probably hiding out and waiting for one of us to find her."

"I'll follow you. But Istaga, you have to make a decision."

Istaga stared at her for a moment and then came close, his arms going tight around her. She felt his heart beating, smelled the sage in his hair. She leaned into him and let the tears fall.

Where they were at this moment was one of the first places they'd ever camped together. But that was before she knew what he was. They'd made love just down the hill from where they were standing and he'd cooked a rabbit over the fire for their breakfast. She hadn't questioned how he'd caught it or why he didn't have words for things, falling under his spell as easily as breathing. So much had changed since then.

Istaga released her and turned toward the mountains, his head back as he sniffed the air. A second later he was on four legs and loping away, his nose to the ground. She wiped away her tears and hurried after him, worrying for a moment about whether or not she could shift again, but when her mind turned to her baby and she felt the love in her heart she found herself on all fours, trotting after him.

≈ৎৡ৯

It was close to dusk before they caught up with the young coyote. Kaliska had found a shallow cave where she could keep out of sight and had curled up in a tight ball, afraid of her own shadow. Coyote found her first, approaching with care. Somehow Sara's coyote brain knew not to shift into human form—at least not right away, and so she crept closer, keeping her belly close to the ground. By the time Sara reached them, Coyote and their pup were sniffing noses and wagging their tails as they greeted. The pup came out of her hidey-hole and approached her mother warily, her eyes narrowed. But once they'd sniffed noses all was well.

Istaga was the first to shift, his eyes on Kaliska as he coaxed her into human form. Sara shifted but stayed back, knowing that the young coyote did not trust her.

When Kaliska didn't shift Istaga turned to Sara. "This happened when I found her a week ago. She'll shift in her own time." Istaga bent to gather some twigs and began to make a fire but neither of them had any matches or way to start it and so he gave up and sat cross-legged, watching the sky.

Sara followed his gaze, awed by the beauty of where they were. Rows of dark conifers climbed the hill in front of them, a deep canyon falling into darkness just ten feet from the cliff face where Kaliska sheltered. Water rushed from a cleft in the hill and fell to join the fast-moving river below. Above the trees the sky was streaked rose, indigo and maroon, stars just winking into view. Sara let out a sigh and lay back, her arms under her head. When Istaga lay next to her she turned. "It's so beautiful here."

Istaga nodded and smiled a secret smile.

❦

Sara was fast asleep when she felt Istaga's hands moving across her body. She responded, rolling against him and finding his mouth. They made love among the stars, the brightness holding and enveloping them as they kissed and explored one another. Sara felt as though everything had come full circle—their love deeper than ever. His long hair lay soft against her cheek, his breath hot in her ear. She relaxed into him, reveling in the beauty of what they were doing and finding within it a sacredness that went far beyond words.

❦

When Sara woke in the morning she was alone. When she called and searched she got no reply and there were no prints to tell her where they'd gone. She waited, hoping Istaga would bring her breakfast as he'd always done in the past, but as the hours rolled by she realized they weren't coming back. And then it occurred to her that she had no way to cook it even if he did return with a rabbit or squirrel.

It was another hour before she decided to find her way home. If Istaga wanted to be with her he would bring their pup and find her. But in her heart she knew the decision had been made. When she thought back to their lovemaking the night before she realized it had been filled with a poignancy that she now recognized as his way of saying goodbye. She wiped at her tears but they wouldn't stop as she left the cave and attempted to retrace her steps back to Black Base.

22

"So what you're saying is Istaga left you there alone and took off with Kaliska? How did you even find your way back?"

Sara stared into Rosie's worried face and then let her gaze drift to the open door she'd just run through. It was nearly midnight—late for Rosie to be up. The denim shirt she always found herself in after shifting was torn and shredded, her bare legs and feet bleeding and scratched from falling on rocks and running through cactus. "It wasn't easy. But I can't stay here with Raleigh and the police looking for me. I don't know what to do."

"You need to lay low, I'll grant you that, but Istaga is more the focus of the manhunt. They've been showing the clips from the Red Lion again on the news, but it's only to rally people against the killer coyote. The only good thing is that Raleigh is severely injured and still in the hospital."

Sara grimaced. "I'm sure he's got his minions spreading the word about Istaga. And from what Istaga told me, Raleigh plans to catch us all and put us in jail until we rot."

Rosie closed the front door and switched on a lamp before grabbing a couple of beers from the fridge. She handed one to Sara and then lowered to the couch.

"Tell me what happened. All I've heard is what Raleigh told the police and the reporters. He said a shape-shifting coyote attacked him and would have killed him if it hadn't been for the police he thought to call when he saw Istaga standing at the side of the road."

Sara twisted the cap off the bottle and took a swig before sitting next to her. "I wondered how the police got there so fast. He had Kaliska in his arms when Raleigh pulled up next to him. But as soon as Raleigh was out of the truck she shifted and took off. I went after her so I missed the rest of it. Istaga told me Raleigh had a gun and was about to shoot him."

Rosie shook her head. "That fact has been sadly missing from the reports. You three have been through enough now. I wish that man were dead."

"That's exactly what I told Istaga." Sara tried to smile. "He was angry at me for saying it after everything that's happened."

Rosie leaned toward her, her gaze intense. "He has a right to be angry, Sara. Anything bad he's done has been to save you."

Sara's anger flared. "I've done nothing but try to help him."

"Is beating him up verbally for killing the man who nearly raped you trying to help him? And what about humiliating him? You may be helping him now, but you weren't a month ago."

"If by humiliation you're talking about denying him sex, we got beyond that. At least I think we did," she added, frowning.

Rosie lifted her brows. "As coyotes or humans?"

Sara's face burned. "Humans. When I think back on it, the entire thing seems like a dream since I was mostly asleep. But earlier I told him that he had to make a decision. I guess he made it."

"Make a decision about what?"

"About whether he loved me enough to live as a human."

"Sara, you didn't, you couldn't..." Rosie looked horrified.

"Why are you looking at me like that? All I said was I couldn't live out in the boondocks anymore. And remember Istaga is now vegetarian. How is he planning to survive?"

"Did you bring that up?"

"Yes, I did. He said he hoped to get over it."

Rosie stared out the window. "Ben told me Istaga came to see him after he jumped out the window that night. He wanted Ben to help him get over his aversion to meat. But in the end Ben helped him find Kaliska instead. Istaga thought if he found your baby you'd be more likely to love him."

"What? Are you serious?"

"That's why he was down on the road that evening. He was bringing your baby back."

Sara thought about their crazy run through the desert, the exhausting climb into the mountains. She'd never thought to ask what he was doing on the road in the first place. Now he was gone again and their daughter with him. "He didn't say a word about that."

"Istaga wants to have a life with you. You told me yourself that when you're together he stays in human form for most of it. What's the problem?"

"He's told me over and over how he only stays human because of me. He hates most humans. If he wanted to have a life with me he wouldn't have left me alone on that mountain."

"Sara, you don't know what prompted him to leave. For all you know Kaliska took off during the night and he went to find her. Don't jump to conclusions. If you were intimate that means..."

"It doesn't mean anything," Sara interrupted.

Rosie went into the kitchen and pulled some covered dishes out of the refrigerator. "Another thing you might want to consider is what happened with Raleigh. The police are searching for Istaga, not you. Istaga knows it would be dangerous for him to show his face around here."

"Why are you making excuses for him? He didn't have to leave me alone up there."

"I make excuses because you always seem to think the worst of him. I don't know what's gotten into you. You used to be a nicer person." Rosie slid the dishes into the microwave and turned it on.

"My baby being gone is what's gotten into me," Sara said. "What are you doing with the food?"

"I'm heating it up. Have you taken a hard look at yourself? You need a meal, a bath and a good night's sleep."

❦

After eating the leftovers Rosie set in front of her Sara took a long bath letting her mind drift over the events of the past few days. She had been so close to having her baby back and now Kaliska was gone again. A feeling of futility went through her at the thought of the two of them out in the wilderness. Istaga had been doing the only thing he knew to get Sara to forgive him and love him again. And now another obstacle had been placed between them. If she could, she'd kill Raleigh herself just to rid him from their lives.

When she stepped out of the tub and saw her body in the full-length mirror she was shocked to see how thin she'd become. Her hips bones jutted, her collarbones too. Each rib was visible, her belly concave beneath her ribcage. Her shoulder length hair was dull and tangled around her pale face and her eyes looked hollow and dark. Lines had formed between her brows and around her mouth.

She stared at her reflection for a long time, trying to come to terms with the person she'd become—angry, unforgiving and controlling with no love left to give. Rosie was right. No wonder Istaga had made the decision to leave her.

23

Coyote howled at the moon, letting his sorrow and frustration out as he stared at the enormous orange ball hanging in the sky above the tree line. Something in him could have kept on howling but just before he opened his mouth again he spied Raven sitting at the top of a large pine tree. He didn't want to hear from the bird right now—didn't want Raven to tell him how stupid he was and how many mistakes he'd made and was still making. All he wanted was to stop whatever was squeezing his chest. He knew coyotes didn't feel like this—knew that the two sides of him were merging into one. He could no longer escape the 'feelings' his human side was having.

He'd taken Kaliska and left Sara at the cave even though they'd coupled and been as close as they'd ever been. He couldn't make sense of why he'd taken off. He only knew that something inside of him could not bow down to her anymore. She made him feel *bad* about himself, a human concept that made him want to curl up and hide. She'd insisted he make a decision but neither choice worked for him. He didn't want to live without her but he could not be stuck where Raleigh and the police could find him. And he also knew that living in one of those structures would make him crazy. And now Kaliska had gone off without him to find another pack. A pain moved through him as these scattered thoughts, like dried leaves in a wind, blew through his animal mind.

"What do you plan to do?" he heard the bird caw. "Stay away from your mate?"

Coyote looked up, meeting the bird's beady eye. "I can't be with her. She's not the same as she was."

"That may be true but it doesn't mean she can't change. She's lost her child, Coyote. To you this means very little but to her it is everything. Kaliska is her heart. She suffers and you have borne the brunt of this because she blames you. You must try and understand the human part of yourself. Without that you will not be able to bridge the canyon that lies between you. And if you do not, you will live out your days wishing and wondering what might have been."

Coyote listened, surprised that for once in his life the bird wasn't berating him. "Kaliska has her own life now. How can I change that?"

"Kaliska is still young. She has not found her mate. There is still time."

"I can't keep taking her away from her pack, Raven. And how do I find her again?"

Raven clacked his beak against the branch and lifted gracefully into the sky. "You know what to do!" he cawed.

Istaga watched where he went, knowing that Raven was showing him the way.

24

*I*t had been a month and a half since Sara's night in the cave with Istaga and Kaliska. She still wasn't sure if what she remembered from that night was true or a dream. Rosie had convinced her that Istaga's disappearance was due to Raleigh and his threats, but it was hard for her to reconcile. Every time she thought about Kaliska and Istaga she felt a pain in the middle of her chest and her eyes would well with tears.

After the last argument with Rosie she'd decided she had to find a place of her own as well as a car. It had taken only a week to find a cheap rental, a trailer on the outskirts of San Manuel, as well as an old Toyota beater that was in good enough shape to get her where she wanted to go.

Her appetite had increased over the last few weeks and she was eating more and seeing a change in her appearance. It was a good thing, since Joe had been horrified at how thin she'd become and threatened to fire her if she didn't start taking care of herself. He told her his customers would worry about what was wrong with her when she waited on them. "Nobody likes to think their waitress is ill or anorexic, Sara."

Tonight she had a date with Rosie to go to the Pig and Pint. They hadn't seen each other in many weeks and Sara was looking forward to music and conversation where she could forget her underlying sadness for a few hours.

When she pulled up to Rosie's house, her friend was waiting for her outside dressed in a fringed leather jacket, jeans and cowboy boots. Sara was dressed similarly but wearing a jean jacket instead of leather, a thick wool scarf wrapped around her neck.

"You look a little better than the last time I saw you," Rosie said, looking her over as she climbed into the car. "You must be eating again."

Sara nodded and leaned over to give her friend a squeeze. "And you look beautiful as always, but even more so. Where did you get that jacket?"

Rosie grinned. "Ben got it for me. He's been coming down on a regular basis."

"Really? How often?"

Rosie lifted her eyebrows. "Every weekend if you can believe it."

Sara put the car in gear and pressed down on the gas, heading toward the main road. It had taken some time to get used to the automatic but now she enjoyed the ease of it. "I'm glad for you two," she said, sliding into the stream of traffic. It was Friday night and there was a band playing at The Pig and Pint. It would be crowded.

అఖ

Inside the bar they found a small table in the back away from where the band had set up and ordered beers.

"So how are you really doing?" Rosie asked her,

leaning forward.

Sara stared into the distance. "I'm ok. Work is keeping me busy and I've been walking. There's a bunch of trails out by the house."

"Ben says that once it's safe he's sure Istaga will come find you."

Sara grimaced. "With Raleigh around it'll never be safe."

The waitress came by and dropped off their beers and then went to the table of five men next to them.

Rosie took a sip of her beer and then plunked the bottle down on the table. "You didn't hear?"

"Didn't hear what?"

"It's been all over the news, Sara. My friend up at the county jail told me."

Sara frowned and leaned forward. "Told you what?"

"Henry, the cop I know, got a call from Duluth. He's been ordered to arrest Raleigh on suspicion of murder."

"What? How did that happen?"

"Henry said some woman named Madeline Harper came forward with evidence regarding her husband's murder a few years back."

Sara took in a breath, staring at her friend. "Are you serious? Madeline is Lee Harper's wife. Lee's the lawyer I told you about, the one who was helping me get away from Raleigh." Sara thought back to being locked up in Raleigh's house and the charade Raleigh expected her to play. His bid for the state legislature had gone nowhere after the news of his affair with

Sara's mother had hit the news. She was already in love with Istaga when she'd escaped from that tomb of a house and headed to Page. "Raleigh sent his thugs after me. It's why I agreed to live out in the boonies for so long. But with Raleigh hanging around here I figured the murder he pinned on me would never go away. This is incredible news!" Sara shook her head, wondering whether to believe it. "Does this mean he'll go to jail?"

"He'll be transported back to Duluth to stand trial. You might be subpoenaed, Sara. I have to tell you that Henry took an instant dislike to Raleigh. He was gleeful when he told me all this, especially with all the hoopla about shape shifters that Raleigh kept going on about. Henry's kind of a salt of the earth type and doesn't believe such a thing is possible."

"I thought he was part native."

"That doesn't mean anything. He is who he is."

Sara let out a whoop. "This is the best news I've heard all year! If only I had some way of reaching Istaga."

"What would you do if he came back?"

At that moment the band began to play and Sara had to lean close to her friend and shout to be heard. "If he brought Kaliska with him I'd greet him with open arms."

"And if he didn't?"

Sara shrugged, turning her attention to the band. In truth she felt horribly guilty for how she treated Istaga and the idea of seeing him made her very nervous. She was sure his reason for leaving her in the cave was solely because of what a bitch she'd become. She understood enough now to realize that her behavior had been directly linked to Kaliska, but if he showed up without their daughter? She wasn't sure what she'd do. Every moment that Kaliska was out there meant more of a chance that she'd never adjust to life as a human child. This realization gnawed at her and kept her awake at night. It made Sara frantic to find her.

"Hey, Sara! Want to dance?"

She looked up at John standing in front of her with his hand out. "Sure," she said, letting him pull her to her feet.

Once the fast dance was over and the band began a slow one, Sara headed toward the table, but John grabbed her, pulling her back to the dance floor.

"So what happened to that weird dude, the one with the yellow eyes?" he asked her, his hand going to her back.

"You mean Istaga—the father of my baby girl?"

John pulled back to stare at her. "He's the father? I thought Raleigh was her father."

"Are you kidding? I originally moved down here to get away from Raleigh. Why would I have a baby with him?"

"You guys are still married. I thought when he blackmailed you into going back to Duluth you two…"

"I would have killed him if he tried."

"So where is your baby?"

Sara gazed over his shoulder. "She's with Istaga."

"Do you see her?"

"No, John. I haven't seen her in almost two

months."

John cocked his head to one side, eyeing her.

"Don't get any ideas, John."

John pulled away and held up both hands in surrender. "I wasn't coming on to you, babe. You aren't my type anymore. You're too damn skinny. Henry was in here the other day and told me he was looking for the dude."

"Raleigh?"

"Yup. I guess some new evidence came to light from the case up north."

"Yeah, Rosie told me. I'm very glad he's gone."

"Hate to tell you this but Henry told me Raleigh took off before he could arrest him. And he isn't up at his cabin. They put out a bolo but so far no sign of him."

The tune ended and Sara pulled away to stare at John. "The bastard's still around?"

John shrugged. "Who knows?"

When Sara got back to the table her mood had turned dark. All the talk about Raleigh and finding out that he'd disappeared made her feel sick to her stomach. She left the table and hurried to the bathroom where she heaved up her beer and the chips she'd eaten.

25

$\mathcal{I}$staga had decided to take Raven's advice. The only humans he had any wish to learn from were Ben and Toh Yah, but this time being with Toh Yah and the other natives appealed more—the rez was far from Black Base and Toh Yah had nothing invested in Istaga's problems nor did he have a relationship with Rosie. For once being far away from Sara made sense to him.

He and Kaliska were traveling toward Page but it was slow going because of his aversion to meat. Sometimes he hitched rides and other times they traveled at night as coyotes. Kaliska hunted while they worked their way north but finding food was always a problem for him.

He had discovered the art of dumpster diving outside restaurants, where leftover bread, salad and vegetables had been tossed. He didn't care how rotten anything was as long as the food didn't contain blood. But it was not enough to sustain him and he began to drop weight and grow weak.

⇦⇨

Istaga was walking down the sidewalk holding Kaliska's hand when a woman stopped him. She was young, wearing a long skirt, cowboy boots, and a loose cotton blouse over her ample chest. Her light brown hair was braided and tied back. "You two look hungry," she said, bending down to ruffle Kaliska's hair. "I live right down the block if you need a home-cooked meal," she said, her kind gray eyes regarding Istaga from under thick dark lashes.

Istaga was surprised by the offer and wondered what the catch was. He'd ended up paying women who offered things like this. "I don't have any money," he told her, trying to move by her on the sidewalk.

"I can always tell the ones who need me," she smiled, touching him on the arm. "I'll cook you a good meal and you can stay under my roof or go on your way. No strings attached."

By now Kaliska had dropped Istaga's hand and grabbed the woman's skirts in her grubby fist. "And this baby needs a bath," the woman continued, lifting Kaliska to rest the baby against her hip.

"I am hungry," Istaga told her. "But why would you trust a strange man?"

"A Native man with a baby?" She scoffed. "Follow me."

That night Istaga ate beans and cheese and tortillas and some kind of shredded vegetable that tasted of lemon and garlic. By the time he'd finished the enormous plate of food Kaliska was already asleep on the couch.

The woman picked up the plates and carried them to the sink. She turned, her gaze going to the sleeping child and then to Istaga. "I don't mind a man in my bed," she told him shyly. "I get lonely."

When Istaga coupled with the woman that night he put all thoughts of Sara out of his mind. He no longer cared what she would think of him or what she'd say. This was on a level that had nothing to do with how he felt about her. And besides, he was sick of feeling bad about himself.

He woke before dawn, pulled on his jeans and shirt and crept into the living room to find Kaliska. She was curled up on the couch in coyote form. He picked her up, opened the door and closed it behind him before he put her on the ground and shifted, the two of them loping away in the pre-dawn light.

The sun was coming up when they shifted again to head down to the road. Istaga hitched a ride north with a truck driver and he and Kaliska climbed into the bed to sit next to cages of chickens and bags of feed. The driver let them out in a small town and took off toward the west.

Istaga was climbing out of a dumpster when a woman happened along, her sympathetic gaze going to the baby playing in the dirt. "Are you two homeless?" she asked.

"We are traveling," Istaga said, pushing a hunk of stale bread into his mouth.

"If you need a place to stay I live close by," she said, glancing at the baby with a worried expression. "And I have better food than that." She pointed to the bread and cabbage in Istaga's hands.

"We do not have far to go," Istaga answered, heading away from her. He thought about the women he'd been with along the way and how kind they all were. He felt bad to turn her down, knew that she needed something from him; he could see it in her eyes. He wasn't like other men—they'd even told him so. They talked and he listened and when they offered themselves he accepted. He never pushed himself on them.

But women were only half the human species. They weren't the ones who hunted coyotes, or killed for no reason other than to see something die. It was the men he couldn't understand.

He picked up his baby and left town behind, heading into the forest. He was on a mission that didn't include the pleasure he got from coupling. The few times he'd allowed it to happen he'd gone away and felt worse, as though being with them had diverted him from his path and possibly done them more harm than good. They were always sad when he left. Sara was his mate and until they decided to part ways forever he didn't want to spend time in other women's beds.

It was nearly three weeks of travel before Istaga and Kaliska reached Toh Yah's village. Istaga remembered where the man's Hogan was and headed up the rock-strewn hill with Kaliska riding on his back. One of the women he'd spent time with had been kind enough to provide him with this metal contraption to carry her and so far it had worked well.

He remembered these dry, sunbaked hills, the silver sheen of the river in the distance, the large manmade lake that provided fishing for the men who came from out of town. And he also knew about the canyons that lay hidden beneath, what the Navajos called 'place where water runs through rocks.' Toh Yah had explained how the water had carved out these caves and tunnels and how dangerous they could be when the rains came. Istaga and Sara had hidden there when the police were after them before Kaliska was born.

"Istaga!"

Istaga looked up to see a dark-haired stocky man coming toward him. He smiled, feeling a weight lift off his heart.

Toh Yah lifted the contraption off Istaga's back and pulled Kaliska free. "What a beauty. Just like her mother," he said, bending down to examine her. "Where is her mother?" he asked, his gaze going to Istaga.

"She's in Black Base."

"And why are you here?"

"It's a long story," Istaga said. "I came to see you."

Toh Yah nodded. "Come on up. We will have a meal and a beer and then we will talk." When he turned and headed away Kaliska ran after him, grabbing the back of his loose-fitting trousers. He picked her up and continued toward his Hogan. Istaga grabbed the baby carrier and hurried after them, surprised to hear Kaliska babbling real words. She'd hardly said anything on the trip and he was afraid she'd forgotten how to speak.

26

It was a month before Sara and Rosie saw each other again, both of them busy with their own lives. Sara was the one who finally broke the silence, calling Rosie on her cell on her way home from the Desert Café.

"Come on down," Rosie urged. "It's Friday and there's a good band playing again. And Ben's here."

"I don't want to horn in on you and Ben!"

"Don't worry about that. We've had so much of each other now we're like an old married couple." Rosie laughed. "Not quite that bad yet, but don't worry about joining us."

Sara met them at the Pig Pint, finding the two of them stuck into a corner table with their heads together. The music hadn't started yet but Rosie and Ben were into their second round of beers.

"Sara!" Ben said, when he saw her. He stood and folded her into a bear- like hug. "You look great!"

Sara smiled and then glanced at Rosie. "Hey, friend. Good to see you."

"Ben's right," Rosie said, looking her over. "You've filled out. And I'm glad to see it!"

Sara sat on the chair Ben pulled out for her. "Not sure how it's happened with all my recent allergies."

"What allergies?"

"I don't know. I'll just eat something and the next

thing I know I'll be

throwing it up." She shrugged, looking around. "Good crowd. Is John here?"

"You want to see John?" Rosie asked with a surprised expression.

Sara laughed. "Actually I asked because I want to avoid him. Speaking of that, have you heard any more news about Raleigh? Have they found him?"

Rosie shook her head. "No sign of him so far. Henry said he must be a good hider since he's got police from every county combing the area for him. More news came through the wire about some other murder he was involved in."

"Really? Who?"

Rosie looked over at Ben. "I shouldn't have said anything."

"Well, you did, so now tell me who it is."

"They found the remains of an older woman who fits your mother's description, Sara. She'd been bludgeoned to death."

Sara's hand went to her mouth and a second later she was running for the bathroom. She retched into the toilet and then flushed and washed her face before heading back to the table. For some reason the image of her mother had done something to her insides and even though they didn't get along it hurt to think of her being dead.

When she came back Rosie stared at her. "I'm really sorry, Sara. I could have prepared you for this kind of news."

"It was just a shock, that's all. I wasn't on good

terms with her but she was still my mother. Where did they find her? Are they sure it's her?"

"They found her body in the woods behind Raleigh's house in Duluth. She was pretty badly decomposed. I guess she'd been buried but some animals dug her up."

"Oh my god." Bile filled her mouth and she nearly had to run for the bathroom again. She swallowed and took in a deep breath. "So it happened a while back."

Rosie nodded. "I wouldn't even know about this if it wasn't for Henry."

The waitress brought Sara's beer and put a plate of fries down on the table. "Who ordered that?" Sara asked.

"Mr. health conscious here," Rosie said pointing to Ben.

Ben grinned sheepishly and popped a fry it into his mouth. "Only time I get to eat stuff like this," he said.

Rosie had ordered nachos, which arrived next, but when Sara took a look at them she felt nauseous again. "This is what I'm talking about," she said, pointing. "I used to love nachos. Right now even looking at them makes me want to retch. And listen to this—last night I absolutely had to have a coke. Do you have any idea how long it's been? I actually drove down to the Circle K to get one."

Rosie stared at her. "How long has this been going on?"

"I don't know—a week or so?"

"Sara, have you had a period since you and Istaga were together?"

Sara blushed, slanting a glance at Ben. "No, but I figured I didn't have enough body fat. I was like twenty pounds under my normal weight. Why?"

"You're pregnant."

Sara shook her head. "No, I'm not. I can't be."

"It's close to three months and with these allergies you're talking about? Allergies don't normally make you throw-up, Sara—not like what you've described. And seriously, your cheeks are pink and your eyes are sparkling. You're definitely pregnant."

Sara shook her head again, frowning. "Crap, I've got to get rid of it," she muttered.

"What are you talking about?"

Sara looked up, meeting Rosie's horrified stare. "If I'm pregnant, and that's a big if, I have to get an abortion. I can't bring another shape shifter into this world. And I'll probably never see Istaga again. How can I raise another coyote baby?" she whispered. "My first one is long gone and so is her father." Sara wiped the tears at the corners of her eyes.

Ben took hold of her hand. "Go find out before you start making plans."

Sara glanced up at him. "Can't you tell me?"

"I'd have to examine you, but it's easy enough to get a kit from the drug store."

"I'd rather not show myself around Black Base and I doubt there's a place in San Manuel to get one. I'd much rather have you tell me."

Ben glanced at Rosie and then turned to Sara. "Come by the house tomorrow. I'll be around."

❧

Sara arrived at Rosie's house a little after eleven in the morning. She figured the two of them would be up and about by then. She'd spent a sleepless night worrying about what to do if Rosie was right and could barely wait to find out the truth. When she knocked on the door she heard Rosie shout, "Ben, can you get it?"

A minute or so later the door opened and Ben stood there wearing only sweat pants. "Did I come too early?"

Ben smiled and shook his head. "Come on in."

The house had a different feel with Ben in residence and there was a woodsy smell Sara recognized from his house up in the mountains. Rosie came out of the bedroom wearing Ben's missing shirt, her feet bare. "Thought you'd come later," she said, moving into the kitchen to make coffee. "Why don't you take her into the bedroom?" she said, looking at Ben. "Unless you want a cup of coffee first." She shot a hostile look toward Sara.

"Jesus, Rosie. Way to make me feel welcome. All you have to say is come back later."

Rosie softened immediately. "Sorry, Sara. We were in the middle of something...not sex," she added, noticing the expression on Sara's face. "It's one of those conversations—you know—the ones you try not to have but have to have in the end?"

"Like the one I never had with Istaga?"

Rosie laughed. "That's the one. Probably a good thing you got here when you did. Ben was about to pack up his things and leave me for good." .

Ben moved toward her and put an arm around her shoulders. "Not so," he said. "But this gives us time to contemplate." He kissed the top of her head. "Follow me, Sara," he said, moving toward the guest bedroom.

"Do I have to take off my clothes?"

Ben shook his head. "I'm going to put my hands on you but nothing invasive, okay?"

Sara nodded. "Should I lie down?"

When Ben nodded she lay back with her head on the pillow. This had been her room for many months and she'd also slept in here with Istaga. She closed her eyes.

At first she didn't feel anything but then she could feel little currents of air moving over and round her body. Ben's hands landed gently on her lower belly and then moved to her middle belly and then touched her breasts lightly before going to cup her face. He pressed his fingers into her temples and began to chant.

Sara wasn't sure if she was awake or asleep and didn't know how long she'd been lying there, but when she opened her eyes Ben was sitting on the side of the bed watching her. "Well?" she asked him, sitting up.

He nodded. "You're definitely pregnant," he told her. "Should come in July, if I'm not mistaken."

"How can you tell? You didn't even give me a pelvic exam."

"Energy, Sara. Your energy has changed. And I could detect the heartbeat."

"But you barely touched me and it seems too early for that."

Ben stood. "I touched you, you just couldn't feel it." He opened the door, went through and closed it behind him.

Sara lay there for a while, contemplating what this meant. A raven-haired little boy came into her mind, reminding her of Istaga with his light-colored eyes and intense expression. She shook her head to clear the vision. She had a momentous decision to make.

When she came into the other room Ben and Rosie had their arms around each other and were lost in a deeply intimate kiss. She was transfixed, wishing she could have this with Istaga. It wasn't just the kiss, it was the way they held each other, their love palpable. When they finally pulled apart their eyes stayed locked together for a long moment before they turned to her.

"Ben told me your news," Rosie said, moving toward Sara. She folded Sara into an embrace. "I hope you decide to keep it, Sara. This baby was conceived in love."

"I know Istaga will be overjoyed when he finds out," Ben added.

Sara shook her head. "I don't expect to ever see him again."

Ben's eyes turned sad. "This coyote you've fallen in love with is a very complex being. He doesn't fully understand the ways of humans or the emotions that plague us. But what I can say for sure is that he loves you and Kaliska as much as he is capable of doing. He will want this being you are carrying and would be heartbroken if you got rid of it."

Sara felt the tears begin and tried vainly to stop

them, but a second later she was sobbing into Rosie's shoulder, her tears staining Ben's denim shirt dark.

Just as she was leaving the house Ben called out, "Keep crackers in your pocket, Sara. It will help with the morning sickness."

Once she was heading home anxiety entered her body like a monster lying in wait. She placed one hand on her lower belly but there was no bulge there, nothing to indicate she was pregnant. And then the child appeared in her mind again, the boy around three years old with Istaga's yellow eyes. He watched her solemnly.

"Stop it!" she yelled. "Go away!" But he didn't and by the time she reached the trailer her thoughts were wild. Why couldn't she get him out of her mind?

27

"So tell me, Coyote-man, what brings you all the way up here?"

Istaga took the beer Toh Yah handed him and settled on the couch next to Kaliska. "It is Raven's words that have brought me here. I need to learn the ways of humans, my lack of understanding has caused what has happened with Sara."

Toh Yah sat next to him and pulled Kaliska onto his lap. The baby let out a happy gurgle and turned to play with the turquoise beads around Toh Yah's neck. "What has happened?"

"She blames me for Kaliska's need to be with coyotes."

Toh Yah's eyes widened. "Sara has not raised this child?"

Istaga shook his head. "At the beginning yes, but then the hunters came and…"

"I am aware of what has been on the news. But you and Sara were together in the video I saw."

"We were and then we were not. I have acted badly and Sara has acted badly. We have hurt each other. I have killed a man and can no longer eat meat."

Toh Yah chuckled and then laughed. "A coyote that can't eat meat?"

"I have tried but it makes me sick."

"And this because you killed a man. Was he a good man?"

"No. He was about to hurt Sara."

"You know this and still you cannot eat meat?"

"Sara was angry. She said I should not have killed him."

Toh Yah nodded. "You will need to sweat these wrong thoughts out of your body and mind."

"I must learn the ways of humans," Istaga said. "Raven said that until I do I won't understand why Sara is so angry."

"This is true. But you are only half human, Istaga. You have an animal side that cannot comprehend the idiocy of the human race."

"But your people are different than others. That is why I came here."

Toh Yah smiled. "We have idiots here too. But our traditions are not like those of the white man. We have a deep bond with the earth and respect what it has to give. Our belief is not to take more than we can use. The white man has grown greedy and takes what he wants with little thought for the coming generations. Do you understand?"

Istaga nodded. "Like the hunters who kill for sport."

"That is correct and that mentality underlies much of what is wrong with the world."

"Sara wants Kaliska to come home and live as a human child, but Kaliska has grown to enjoy her freedom. I have told Sara that as a coyote Kaliska is full grown now and has a right to be on her own."

Toh Yah gazed at the child in his lap. "Humans keep their babies close for many years, Istaga--too many, in my opinion. But you have to remember that a coyote's life is very short in comparison to a human. Human babies need mother's milk for a year or more and then protection until they leave home at eighteen. Coyotes nurse their young for only a couple of months and then teach them to hunt. By the time a human child has left home a coyote has lived his entire life and died. Kaliska is still very young in human years. What is her wish?"

Istaga thought about what Toh Yah had said, trying to sort through the information that he didn't fully understand. If Kaliska stayed coyote she would die sooner than he would as Istaga. A pain came into his body as he imagined her death. "She has been in the wild and traveled with a pack, but on this trip she has spent many hours in human form. I could tell she enjoyed the attention she got from the women I met along the way."

Toh Yah raised his eyebrows. The baby was babbling to herself in her secret language but every time her name was mentioned she looked up. "Kaliska lives in both worlds, but neither one have claimed her fully. Is that how you want to live, Istaga, in both worlds? Or just in one?"

"Sara doesn't want to live out in the wild anymore. She wants her human life. And her former mate, Raleigh, is still around and wants to put Kaliska and me in jail. "

"Raleigh is in Black Base? I thought he lived in the

north somewhere."

"He did but he decided to join the predator masters and now he has a cabin in the mountains near Black Base."

"So the reality is that you cannot be in Black Base and Black Base is where Sara wants to live. I'd say you have a big problem."

Istaga hung his head, feeling defeated. Said like that it clarified how impossible the situation was. "Everything was so simple with the women I met on the way here," he muttered, looking down.

"These chance encounters are easy, Istaga. It is the long term relationships that are difficult, especially when one is a coyote and the other human."

"And if I am at heart a coyote will I die when my coyote side dies?"

"That is an interesting question. If this body you inhabit is truly human then I would say no, you would live a longer life."

"But I go back and forth all the time. What will this do to me?"

Toh Yah put his hand on Istaga's shoulder. "I cannot answer that. You must discover this on your own. Do not be discouraged. I've managed to fix situations a lot worse than this."

Istaga tried to smile, thinking about the day Sara turned into a coyote for the first time. It had happened here in this village. Without Toy Yah and the other villagers' kindness the police would have caught them. He watched the baby playing with Toh Yah's beads, a look of concentration on her face. "I lost the beads you gave me," he told Toh Yah, his hand going to his bare neck.

Toh Yah slipped the baby off his lap and went to the counter in the kitchen. "These beads?" he asked, holding up the strand he'd given Istaga years before.

"So it *was* you I saw."

Toh Yah smiled and brought the beads over, handing them to Istaga. "I've been with you a time or two."

28

Sara's morning sickness got worse rather than better as the days went by. She did as Ben told her but even the saltines she kept with her didn't alleviate the sudden need to throw up. Work was nearly impossible with her having to run to the bathroom between customers, her face pale and sweaty.

"Do you have the flu?" Joe finally asked her, reaching out to touch her forehead. "I don't want you working with food if you're sick."

"I'm pregnant," she told him reluctantly. "I'm trying to decide if I should keep it or not."

Joe stared at her for a full minute without speaking, finally asking, "Whose baby is it?"

"It's Istaga's," she said. "I haven't slept with anyone else."

Joe seemed to relax. "Glad to hear that. I didn't want to think about you…"

"Whoring around? You must have a really warped idea of who I am."

"Hard to know who you are, Sunny, with you telling me you have some checkered past that you refuse to reveal. And your baby is still gone? You don't seem that upset about it anymore."

"My baby is with her father."

"So Istaga is not with you? How did you get

pregnant?"

Sara let out an exasperated sigh. "We've been together off and on."

"If the baby is Istaga's why would you consider an abortion?"

Sara watched a family of four come through the door and seat themselves. "Because I don't know if we'll ever be together again." Sara wiped her eyes and went to hand menus around, glad to be finished with the conversation.

❧

"Sara, are you feeling good enough to come out tonight?"

Sara listened to Rosie's voice on the cell phone, her mind on many other things. She was home from work and had just poured herself a beer, rationalizing drinking alcohol with the idea that she wouldn't be keeping the baby anyway. "Is Ben there?"

"No, he went home. We're taking a little break."

Sara heard the catch in her friend's voice. "What time should I meet you?" she asked.

❧

It was close to eight by the time Sara reached Rosie's house. As soon as she stopped the car the door opened and Rosie appeared dressed in a warm coat and boots. Sara had the heat cranked in the car and still she was shivering. There had been an unusual dip in the temperature and many of the prickly pears had died.

Rosie came around to the passenger side and slid

inside, pulling the door shut behind her. "It's freezing!"

"Joe said the cold snap is only supposed to last a couple of days. I hope he's right."

"Does he still think your name is Sunny Sullivan?"

"I haven't told him anything different. He already thinks I'm nuts."

Rosie laughed. "Why?"

"I've been evasive about my past—strangely enough I didn't want to tell him Istaga is really a coyote--and when I told him I was pregnant he assumed I was a prostitute or something. When I said it was Istaga's he couldn't understand why I would consider an abortion."

"Jesus, Sara, that again? It's getting kind of late for it now. Aren't you more than three months?"

Sara shrugged. "I don't know what to do—that's the reason I haven't done anything yet. I keep hoping Istaga will show up, but a part of me knows it's crazy to think like that." She pulled away from the curb and headed onto the road leading toward the bar.

"Who knows? Ben seems to think he will."

"What's going on with you and Ben?" Sara asked, trying to change the subject.

Rosie let out a sigh and stared into the dark night. "We want to live together but it's impossible with him up there and me down here. We can't seem to come up with a compromise."

"Sounds familiar," Sara said, glancing at her friend. "You would have to quit your job, right? Why won't he move down here?"

"Can you see Ben down here full time? He's a

mountain man, Sara. He couldn't survive in an urban area like this."

"Seems like you had it worked out with him coming for weekends."

"We both want more."

"This sounds so familiar that it gives me the shivers--Istaga and his need to live in the wild and my need to be around people."

"The only difference is you gave him an ultimatum. Ben and I are trying to come up with a solution that works for both of us."

"That's a mean thing to say, Rosie. Ben doesn't have your baby up there, now does he?"

"You have to admit you didn't give him much choice. And another thing, as long as we're on the subject—if I were pregnant with Ben's child I would never, ever consider having an abortion. I love him too much."

Sara slammed her foot on the brake and pulled over to the side of the road, scattering gravel. "That is totally uncalled for! I'm living on my own in an f--ing trailer! How am I supposed to raise a baby that could be a shifter? Jesus, Rosie—you can't equate what I'm going through with you and Ben."

Rosie looked down for a moment. "I'm sorry, Sara. You're right. I'm upset about my own situation and I'm taking it out on you." She reached over and took hold of Sara's hand. "Will you forgive me?"

Sara nodded. "We're both having a hard time right now. I wish we could help each other rather than being adversaries."

"Let's go listen to some music. Maybe it'll cheer us up."

❧

Sara danced with several strange men and drank too many beers as she tried to let go of the decision she needed to make. But after she dropped Rosie off and was on her way home the tears began. If she didn't do something soon it would be too late.

Rosie had made her promise to call if she decided to go through with it, saying, 'no woman should have to go through that kind of procedure alone.'

She went to bed with the decision on her mind, her thoughts turning as they always did to Istaga and Kaliska. Would she ever see her baby girl again?

Sara was walking through woods that were unfamiliar with the sound of birds she didn't recognize and trees that didn't grow in Arizona. It was quiet, the expectation of something hovering in the air as though waiting. Sara wasn't nervous although she knew she should be. There was something dangerous here, something that clung to the mists between the trees. When she arrived at a pool of water she stripped off her clothes and climbed in, surprised to find the water warm and soothing. She lay back and closed her eyes.

A sudden sound startled her and when she opened her eyes Istaga was in the pool with her. He said nothing as he reached for her. They kissed and then his hands moved across her body in a practiced way, his eyes glittering gold as he watched her reactions to what he was doing. There was something wrong here, something that didn't make sense, but before she could puzzle it out they were mating like animals and she couldn't pull away. A sudden fear had her pulling back to see him, realizing in a horrible moment of clarity that it was not Istaga, it was Raleigh, and he had shifted into a coyote, his teeth bared ready to sink them into her neck.

Sara woke screaming, her hand going to her throat. She was shaking all over, her heart beating wildly. A flutter went through her midsection and she put both hands there. She lay in the dark trying to figure out what the dream was trying to tell her but nothing she thought about made any sense. She finally fell into a fitful sleep.

In the morning Sara felt as though she hadn't slept at all, her mind still on the dream. It was when she was making coffee that she noticed a shadow move by the window. When she opened the door to check she noticed a truck parked next to her car in the driveway. It was red. And a second later she saw Raleigh coming toward her with a gun in his hand.

29

Istaga was in the sweat lodge with Toh Yah and several other men. He had left the baby with Haseya, a native women who he'd met in the past who assured him she wouldn't let Kaliska out of her sight.

What was he supposed to get out of this? It was just another human ceremony that made no sense to him. He had not eaten in a long time and felt weak and shaky. The smoke from the sage Toh Yah kept throwing on the fire filled his nostrils making him cough.

"Let your spirit float, Istaga," he heard Toh Yah say. "Allow all the thoughts of bad and good to disappear inside the smoke and lift up and out, into the sky. You must cleanse and purify in order for the Great Spirit to enter and give you the answers you seek. It is hard to be coyote and man at the same time. Which side will you embrace? To be with the woman requires a pure heart, one that understands. Can you understand?"

Istaga looked at Toh Yah, wondering if he was supposed to answer this question but Toh Yah's eyes were closed, the question hanging in the air as though the spirits would answer. When Istaga closed his eyes he saw Sara. Yes, he wanted more than anything to be with her, but there was something dark that lay between them. She wanted him to be different than he was. Should he change to be with her?

This question was answered as Toh Yah said, "Be true to yourself. Without that there is nothing."

But what was his truth? Was he coyote? Man? He didn't understand and as the sweat dripped from his brow he became more and more confused. At one point he thought he'd shifted, surprised to look down and see that he was still Istaga. And then the sweat was over and Toh Yah had opened the flap, letting in the frigid air.

"What did you discover?" Toh Yah asked him later when they were back in the Hogan. Toh Yah stood at the chopping block, using his knife to slice up carrots and other root vegetables to make soup.

Istaga was sitting cross-legged next to Kaliska who played on the floor with several long strands of dark colored beads Toh Yah had given her. Istaga pulled his gaze away from her and looked up. "I discovered nothing."

Toh Yah laughed. "Nothing could contain everything. Tell me what you experienced during the sweat."

"I was hot and water poured out of my skin. I thought I had shifted but I had not. I thought of Sara but I knew that she did not want me as I am. I was confused."

"Did your thoughts of bad and good leave you?"

"I no longer have those, but now there is nothing inside to guide me."

"Do you think you need the idea of bad and good

to guide you?"

"It seems to be what humans use to show them what to do."

Toh Yah nodded. "In many cases this is true and it is a problem. Humans are not in touch with their inner light and they expect someone from the outside to tell them how to act. It is why religion is so important to many of them. But the god they worship is not the god I see when I walk in the mountains."

"I have not been to the structures that claim to be in touch with this person. Sara does not believe in it."

"But she does believe in good and bad. Bad is when you killed a man to save her life."

Istaga stared at the floor. "She was mad at me for something else."

"Very good, Istaga. You are beginning to understand humans."

30

"How did you find me?" Sara, asked, backing away from the gun pointed at her midsection.

Raleigh shifted the gun to his other hand and adjusted his cowboy hat. In Sara's opinion he looked ridiculous, as though he was playing dress-up for a comedy routine having to do with incongruous cowboys.

"I told that man you work for that I was your husband. He told me where you lived."

"What do you want from me, Raleigh?"

Raleigh followed her inside, the gun waving as he spoke. "I want you dead or in jail. You're an abomination."

"You're the one who should be in jail. I just found out you killed my mother."

Raleigh laughed. "Candace had it coming. She wouldn't leave me alone."

"No one has it coming, Raleigh, I don't care what she did. You took advantage of a woman who was terrified of getting old."

Raleigh shook his head. "You're kidding, right? She was damned lucky I let her seduce me."

Sara stared at him, wondering how she ever could have tolerated him. "So how did it happen? Did you just decide one day to smash her head in?"

"She pushed me too far, Sara. It just happened."

"And you thought no one would discover her body? Her body was found on your property."

"She's been there for a couple of years. How did I know they were going to be combing the area again?"

Sara glanced out the window, surprised to see two deer run by. She heard a gunshot and then another. "The hunters are out there. Don't you want to join them in their killing spree?"

When Raleigh turned to look out the window Sara grabbed the gun out of his hand and took off out the door. She hurtled toward the forest of mesquite trees, her heartbeat loud in her ears. She didn't look back, but she heard his heavy footsteps as he pounded after her. She wound her way along trails that she knew now, ones that were not well trodden where she hoped to lose him.

The hunters were in here, she could hear shots in the distance, and she was pretty sure this was a no hunting zone since it was near a residential housing area. She hoped she wouldn't be mistaken for one of the poor animals they were trying to kill. When another shot rang out she crouched down, sure that she'd felt a bullet zing by her ear. She waited and then made her way deeper into the trees.

It was about five minutes later that she heard shots very close to where she was hiding, followed by the unmistakable scream of a human being. A moment passed and then another before three men in camouflage ran by. Their baseball caps had the familiar logo that identified them as part of the predator masters. She heard shouting and another scream, this one high and full of pain.

Sara waited another fifteen minutes before she took a circuitous trail back toward the trailer. By the time she reached the door she heard sirens in the distance.

❧

"Did your husband find you?" Joe asked Sara when she arrived at the Desert Café the next morning.

Sara looked up from where she was taking off her work boots. "That man is not my husband."

Joe frowned. "He insisted you were married. Who is he?"

Sara let out a sigh and pushed her feet into her comfortable flats. "I hate to admit this, but we're still married. I could never manage to get a divorce."

"Is that the baggage you've been holding back?"

"Part of it," Sara answered, shrugging.

"I have to say he didn't seem like your type. I hope I didn't get you into trouble."

"Actually, Joe, you did me a huge favor." Sara smiled, thinking about the ambulance that carried Raleigh's body away. She'd checked with the hunters who'd called 911 and they admitted that they'd accidentally shot a man who was wearing a brown leather jacket and a cowboy hat, and that there was only a slim chance he would live. After that conversation she'd made it clear that they were not welcome here and told them she would report them to the police if she heard any more shooting.

The heavier of the two had paled, his words of 'we

thought he was a deer,' high-pitched and frightened. When the police arrived and took the three men away Sara had closed and locked her door, leaning against it as she tried to let go of the adrenaline.

"So this Istaga fellow is the father of your little girl and your unborn child?"

"That's right. He has long dark hair and looks Native American. So if someone else comes in claiming to be my husband who doesn't look like that, don't believe him."

Joe's eyes widened. "There are others?"

Sara laughed. "I'm kidding, Joe."

Joe shook his head and went to start the hash browns while Sara set up the tables in the front.

❧

It was when she arrived home after work that Sara began to process the events of the night before, realizing how close she'd come to being killed or dragged off to jail. And now the very hunters he had joined had shot Raleigh. The irony of it made her laugh. But she also felt sad that things had gotten this far out of hand. She picked up her cell and dialed Rosie's number.

"Have you decided to do it?" Rosie asked.

"I'm not calling about that, Rosie. There was an incident out here last night. Raleigh was shot. Have you heard anything about it?"

Rosie was silent for a moment. "No, I haven't. Do you need me to check with Henry?"

"They took Raleigh to the hospital. I just wanted to

see if he lived or died."

"Sara, did you shoot him?"

"No, but I wish I had. The only problem would have been the gun I would have used—his. And my fingerprints would have been all over it."

"How did he get shot?"

"You won't believe it—it was the hunters who are part of that group he belongs to. Ironic, don't you think? The police took the three guys away. Maybe they'll have to stand trial."

"I'll call Henry and call you back, okay?"

"Sounds good."

Sara hung up the phone and pulled a beer out of the fridge. She popped the cap off and took a long pull and then settled down on the couch with her feet up. She'd heard from several sources that beer was good for pregnant mothers.

When the phone rang a few minutes later she was in a reverie in which she, Istaga, and their two children were playing house in a log cabin that opened into wilderness. One entire side of the building was open to the elements, a bank of French doors between that and the rest of the house. It was the perfect compromise. But a place like that was not in her price range, she thought, looking around the shabby space she was renting.

"Raleigh is dead," Rosie announced when Sara picked up. "They pronounced him DOA at the hospital."

Sara couldn't speak for a moment. "I don't know whether to laugh or cry."

"Laugh, you silly girl! He's finally out of your hair for good. Istaga can come back now."

"If only I could call him on a cell phone and tell him the news."

Rosie chuckled. "Have you ever noticed how psychic he is? I bet you he turns up in the next week or two. Now, Sara, what have you decided?"

Sara felt another flutter in her belly and placed a hand there. "It's too late to do anything now," she answered.

"That is a cop out and you know it. If you're keeping the baby then say so. Don't pretend it's the absence of a decision."

Sara chuckled. "I'm keeping it, okay? The little bastard's been plaguing me. How could I do anything else?"

"What in god's name do you mean by that?"

"I've seen this baby when he's around three years old and he looks just like Istaga, including that intense expression he gets—you know the one."

"You've seen him--do you mean inside your head, at a playground—or what?"

"In my head, Rosie. He appears to me."

"Okay. This is getting weird. I think I'll hang up now. I'm glad you've decided to keep the baby, though."

"Before you hang up, what about you and Ben?"

"Haven't seen him."

When Sara began to respond she saw that the call had ended. She chuckled to herself about Rosie's reactions. The woman accepted a shape-shifting coyote but couldn't deal with Sara having a psychic connection with her unborn child?

Sara finished her beer, suddenly aware of a lift in her spirits. Maybe it was the idea of no more Raleigh, maybe it was the decision to keep the baby—or possibly she believed what Rosie said about Istaga. He was psychic in his own way, either that or it was purely coyote instinct, but whatever it was, she had a feeling he would be back and that Kaliska would be with him. She went to bed that night with a smile on her face for the first time in a year.

31

*I*staga had been with Toh Yah for nearly three months, following the man around and helping out with building, farming and whatever other ways in which he could be of use. He'd learned how to turn the earth and plant the tiny seeds and care for them, watching when the green appeared on the surface of the dark earth. He'd felled trees in the forest and stripped them to use for building the log houses many of the tribe lived in. He'd learned to work the machines that made the logs into boards and used hammer and nails to put them together.

There was something that felt good about being here with these people. He never worried that they might turn on him or treat him badly or head out with their weapons to slaughter animals just for the fun of killing. And they accepted him as he was. He thought about Sara every day, but he knew that until he could truly understand humans there was no point in trying to make things work between them. And with Raleigh looking for him it was safer to be here.

"If you were not who you are I would suggest an initiation ceremony," Toh Yah told him as they walked up the hill to Haseya's Hogan to retrieve Kaliska.

"The spirit quest?"

Toh Yah chuckled. "Sending you out into the

wilderness would not achieve much."

When Kaliska saw the two men approaching she wriggled out of Haseya's arms and ran toward them. Istaga scooped her up and swung her high in the air, her giggles lifting into the bright cloudless sky. When he placed her on the ground she grabbed Toh Yah's trousers and lifted her arms to be picked up. The older man swung her onto his shoulders and waved goodbye to Haseya before they retraced their steps toward his Hogan.

"What is it that you hope to learn here, Istaga?"

Istaga pondered the question. "How to make Sara love me again," he finally said.

"And bringing Kaliska back to Sara is not enough?"

Istaga shrugged, a gesture he had recently learned that seemed to suggest confusion. "I cannot take her back if I am wanted by the police."

Toh Yah's gaze went toward the mountains. "It's been three months. Perhaps Raleigh has gone."

Before Istaga could answer an enormous raven took Istaga's attention. The bird was focused on him and when he met the beady stare something inside him stirred to life. He felt the message enter his heart as though words were being spoken. Once the bird lifted on strong wings and flew away Istaga turned to Toh Yah. "Raleigh is dead," he said.

Toh Yah nodded as though he knew this already, and then headed inside the Hogan. "The universe is looking out for you, Coyote-man. I would take this as a sign that it is safe for you to go back. But can you compromise now?"

"I do not understand the meaning of that word."

"It means giving up some of your needs in order to get along with another. Sara has told you she is not willing to live in the wilderness, but are you willing to live in a house?"

Istaga glanced at Kaliska playing with the small teddy bear Toh Yah had given her. He was surprised by how she had taken to life here. She hadn't shifted since they arrived and played happily with the simple things Toh Yah provided her with. Perhaps human life would work out after all. But then he remembered the feeling of being closed inside the structures humans used. Here he took a sleeping bag and slept outside under the stars, but if he and Sara were together that would never work. "I cannot live inside a structure."

"If you cannot come to an agreement with Sara you will not solve your problem. No amount of learning about human ways will change how you feel. You are still essentially animal."

Istaga knew this was true. This problem had kept him awake at night. "But I must take the baby back even if we cannot bridge the canyon that lies between us," he said, quoting Raven's words.

Toh Yah smiled. "Very poetic, but more importantly you now understand Sara's need to be with her baby despite what happens with the two of you. You are willing to give up something you want in order to make Sara happy. This is a big step, Istaga. You are ready to move on."

Toh Yah went into the back room, reappearing with a rounded piece of wood with holes in it. "I made this for you." Toh Yah put it to his lips and began to play, his fingers moving from hole to hole. The lilting sounds made Istaga's chest ache, water welling in his eyes.

"This is in the key of F♯ and corresponds to the heart. When you play this flute it will open your heart and help you understand the things you find confusing. I will teach you the basics but after that you must play what comes to you."

The fetish, tied on with a piece of leather, covered the sound hole. Istaga learned that it had to be placed just so in order for the sound to be right. His fetish was in the shape of a coyote. Toh Yah had painted a raven on the bottom of the flute with a band of tiny turquoise pieces imbedded around the base where the bird seemed to perch.

It was two weeks before Istaga could train his fingers to cover the holes properly and how to move them in a way that kept the pure sound from becoming distorted. It was another week before he could play anything that didn't hurt his ears.

Over the next turning of the moon Istaga helped finish building a small house for one of the tribe members. When it was completed he decided it was time to head back to Black Base. The day he told Toh Yah the older man didn't seem surprised. "It's spring now and the weather is right for your travels."

Two days later Istaga had packed the clothes the Native women had donated for Kaliska, adding his own clothing to the pack. He put on the heavy coat Toh Yah had given him and pulled the hand-knitted wool sweater over his daughter's blonde curls. He paused outside the Hogan to say his good-byes feeling a strange squeezing sensation inside his chest.

"The pine nuts are ready now and I have shown you how to pick them," Toh Yah told him, handing him a pack of food. "If Kaliska wishes to hunt allow her the freedom to do so. She must decide what she wants her life to be." Toh Yah clasped Istaga close for a long moment. "Look for me when you have questions. I will always be around."

Istaga nodded, put Kaliska in her carrier and hoisted her onto his back. He slung the backpack over his shoulder. "Thank you, Toh Yah. I will miss you."

Toh Yah grinned. "That is a very human thing to say, Istaga. You have learned well."

◆◆◆

Istaga hitched a ride with a trucker for the first leg of the trip, taking the route 89 down to the town of Flagstaff. He remembered the numbers from the first time he'd traveled to Page. From Flagstaff he knew how to get to Black Base on foot.

Kaliska kept up a steady stream of chatter, making the driver laugh. "She's a talker, isn't she? Too bad no one can understand a word she says."

"It is a secret language," Istaga said, repeating what he'd heard from Sara and others. He pulled out his flute for a while, trying out some of the fingerings he'd taught himself.

"What tribe are you from?" the man asked once Istaga put the flute away. "That girl of yours does not resemble you in any way."

The look the man gave him and the way he said this gave Istaga a nervous feeling in his stomach. "Her mother has sun hair and sky eyes."

"Don't you Indians usually stick with your own kind?"

Istaga didn't know what to say to this. "You can let us off here," he said, glancing out at the pine forest stretching to the southeast.

The trucker pulled into a rest area. "I hope you didn't kidnap that little girl," he said, watching Istaga suspiciously.

At that moment Kaliska let out a happy chortle and threw her arms around Istaga's neck. "Would she act like this if she was not my pup?"

The trucker shook his head. "You talk weird. Get on then," he said, gesturing to the door.

Istaga opened the door and pulled Kaliska after him before retrieving her pack and his other backpack. "Thank you for the ride."

He watched the man back the semi and drive away. He'd forgotten about this aspect of humans. Why did they always think the worst? Did he look that untrustworthy? He grabbed Kaliska, fitted her into the pack and onto his back before he picked up the backpack, glad that he wouldn't be hitching any more rides.

✧

Cold weather and the white rain came a day later, making it impossible to travel. He and Kaliska shifted and huddled together in a cave, watching the silent flakes come down and close them in. Luckily they had the food Toh Yah had provided and thick fur to keep them warm.

Three days later they were on two legs and on their way again, following the animal trails through the forest. Kaliska did not shift, as if her stay on the rez had reinforced the human side of her. Istaga was happy when she made no attempt to hunt. He didn't relish the idea of her disappearing into the woods and having to search her out. So far he hadn't heard any coyote calls, but he knew there were packs living around here. He'd seen them on past trips. And then his mind went to the predator hunters, wondering if they were back. It could explain the shots he'd heard in the distance and the lack of wildlife.

It was several turnings of the sun before Istaga began to recognize his former hunting grounds. When he and Kaliska stopped beside a creek to rest and eat some of the pine nuts he'd collected they were only a day's walk from Black Base. The temperatures had risen as they came down out of the hills. Birds were calling and making nests. He was attempting to imitate the calls on his flute when he noticed Kaliska suddenly shift, her hackles raised in alarm. A second later she was running through the brush.

Istaga hid their belongings and shifted to go after her. When he caught up she was hiding in an opening that appeared to be an abandoned mine. Her eyes were wide with terror. On the cliff above he saw what had caused her sudden fear. A mountain lion stared down, long tail swishing as it prepared to jump. Coyote grabbed the pup in his jaws and backed up, his attention on the actions of the cat. Once he'd put some distance between them he shifted into Istaga and grabbed the pup around her middle. The cat looked wary when it saw the human standing there and a few moments later it melted into the brush.

Istaga carried the pup back to where he'd left their things, wondering how to get her to shift into Kaliska. She was not very obedient when it came to these sorts of things. He put her down and took off his belt and hooked it around her neck, his foot on the end to keep her close. "If you will not shift I will have to treat you like a dog," he said, pulling his flute out of the pack. He played for a while, letting the eerie notes float up, watching the colors they made as they moved through the trees. His heart felt full, as though the music filled the hollow place he always carried. Inside the music was something he couldn't identify, a feeling that reminded him of his early days as Istaga when he and Sara were first together. He was unsure, nervous about seeing her again. He had no idea how she felt now or what to expect. The only thing he knew for sure was how happy she would be to have Kaliska back. He imagined leaving Kaliska with her and taking off on his own, the idea of it bringing water to his eyes.

When he bent to put away his flute Kaliska was lying at his feet fast asleep. He picked her up, wrapped her in a blanket and gently put her into the carrying pack. When he hoisted it onto his back she was still sleeping soundly. He slung the backpack over his shoulder and moved on. With any luck they would make it to Black Base before the light left the sky.

32

"Sara, how long do you plan on working?"

Sara looked over at her boss before placing the dish she'd just washed in the drainer. "What do you mean?"

"I mean you're getting big. I don't want to end up delivering this baby."

Sara laughed. "I'm many months away from that, Joe. I'm only six months."

Joe's eyes went wide. "Are you carrying twins?"

"I don't know—I don't think so."

"Sara, don't tell me you haven't gone to the doctor."

"Why do I need a doctor? I'm just having a baby."

"Didn't you go with the first one?"

Sara shook her head thinking back to Kaliska's birth. As always, just the thought of her daughter made her eyes well with tears. She'd given up on ever seeing her again. "No, I never did." That birth had happened in a cave, a fact she would never share with Joe.

"Don't you want to know if it's a girl or a boy?"

"It's a boy."

"And how do you know that?"

Sara grinned. "I just do. In answer to your first question, I plan to work for as long as I can. I feel great." Except for the crying jags she had nearly every night wishing she could share this time with Istaga.

And Kaliska's absence was an ache in her heart that never went away.

❧

On her way home from work Sara's cell phone rang. She answered when she saw Rosie's name on the screen.

"Want to come out tonight? It's Friday and there's a band playing."

"I'm as big as a house, Rosie. I hardly have any clothes that fit."

"Come on by and I'll lend you one of my dresses from when I was fat."

"You were fat?"

Rosie scoffed. "I weighed two-hundred pounds."

"When was this?"

"After my husband was killed I kind of went on an eating binge."

"That's hard to imagine," Sara replied thinking about Rosie's perfect body.

Sara hung up after promising to come early enough to try on one or two of Rosie's dresses.

❧

"That one looks great on you," Rosie said, standing back to assess her.

The dress was a pale lilac color, slightly fitted in the bust area, the skirt billowing out to cover her protruding belly. She stuck her hands in the two large pockets on either side. "You could wear this, Rosie. The style would look good on a thin person."

"I haven't worn any of those clothes since I lost the

weight. They remind me too much of how I felt during that time."

"I totally get that." Sara looked at herself in the mirror, surprised by how pretty she looked. Her hair was down to her shoulders now and shiny, and her skin glowed. "Wow. I love it. But it's probably kind of dressy for the Pig and Pint."

Rosie chuckled. "Pregnant ladies get to wear whatever they like."

❧

It was late by the time Sara headed home. She'd enjoyed herself more than she expected and actually danced a little. But as soon as she was on the dark road that led toward the trailer the sadness returned. She missed Kaliska and Istaga, her heart closing down as she tried not to cry. Her expectations about their imminent arrival had disappeared over a month ago and now she was resigned to bringing this baby up by herself.

She parked the Toyota under the trees and followed the moonlit path toward the front door, her keys in her hand. But when she got there the door was standing open. Sara stopped and backed up slowly, pulling her cell out to call the police, but then she heard something that made her heart stop. It was the giggle of a baby. "Who's there!" she called out, poised to run.

A dark head poked out the door and then Istaga appeared, his eyes shining in the moonlight as he came toward her.

"What are you...how did you find me?"

But before she could say anything else he had enfolded her in his arms, his breath warm on her neck. She smelled the scent of sage and pine in his hair, felt his arms strong around her body, the beat of his heart against hers. When they pulled apart he looked down at her belly, his expression confused. "You...you have been with another man." He backed away, a frown forming between his dark brows.

"Istaga, this is your baby. It happened the last time we were together."

Istaga stopped and stared at her. "Mine."

"Yes." Sara waited for a moment to let that sink in and then moved past him, heading inside. She switched on the light to see Kaliska nestled into her bed. A second later she had the baby in her arms.

It was only a few seconds before Kaliska began to wriggle, letting out a howl of frustration. Sara released her and pushed the hair back from her baby face. "You've grown so much, my sweet one. Do you remember me?"

Kaliska reached up to take hold of Sara's hair. "Mama," she said.

A hand came on Sara's shoulder and she turned, meeting Istaga's tear-filled eyes as he glanced down at her belly. "Raven let me know that Raleigh was gone. I would have come sooner."

Sara stared at him, aware once again of his connection to the spirits and nature around him. It had always mystified her when he reported these sorts of things. "Raleigh is gone for good, Istaga. He's dead." And then she put her arms around him and pulled him close, the three of them huddling together as though it was their last moment on earth.

֍

It was sometime in the night when Istaga kissed her ear and drew her close. His hands moved across her belly. "This baby is big," he said. "It must be a male."

Sara nodded and then murmured, *yes*, into his ear. "I have seen him. He looks like you."

Istaga laughed. "When will he come?"

"Four turnings of the moon, I think. It will be during the hot time." And then she turned and kissed him.

֍

When Sara woke, the baby was still asleep next to her, but Istaga was not in the bed. When she rose and looked out the window she spotted a dark shape just outside the garden under the palo verde tree. She left the baby sleeping and hurried outside. When she placed a hand on his arm he rolled over and opened his eyes.

"When did you leave?" she asked.

He smiled sleepily and rubbed his eyes. "After we mated and you fell asleep. I cannot sleep inside."

"I have to go to work soon. Will you be okay on your own for a few hours?"

When Istaga nodded and pushed himself up she noticed how much his body had changed. His shoulders were wider, his arms muscled and strong. She took hold of his arm. "Your body is different—

bigger than I remember."

"I learned how to build a house, how to chop wood, how to grow vegetables."

Sara stared at him, surprised. "You lived with Toh Yah?"

He nodded. "But I slept outside in a sleeping bag."

"No Coyote?"

He shook his head and pulled his hair back, tying it with the leather he pulled out of his jeans pocket. "No Coyote."

≪❧≫

Sara left Istaga in charge of Kaliska and went to dress, smiling when she heard the baby announce loudly that she wanted cereal for her breakfast. She was amazed by Kaliska's vocabulary as well as Istaga's ability to deal with her human needs. She watched him get out the carton of milk and add it to the cereal he'd poured into a bowl. He handed her a spoon, which she seemed to know how to use.

On the way to work she went over the night's events, coming to the conclusion that there was something making her uneasy, but she didn't know what it was.

Joe let her off early after she told him that Istaga had arrived. She left the Desert Café and hurried to the market to buy food and then headed home. When she got there the door was open but no one was inside. While putting her groceries away she heard the sound of a flute wafting from under the mesquite trees some distance from the house. She pulled a shawl around her shoulders and headed out to find him.

Kaliska was sitting in the dirt playing with the bean pods from the mesquite tree while Istaga sat cross-legged playing a beautiful Native flute. "When did you learn how to play the flute?" she asked, crouching next to him.

He stopped playing and turned. "Toh Yah taught me. He made this one." He handed it to Sara who looked it over, noticing the hand carved coyote fetish and the ring of turquoise shards embedded around the bottom—a perch for the dark eyed raven who peered out from the rounded wood.

"It's beautiful," she said, handing it back.

Istaga slipped it into a woven bag. "Do you wish to go for a walk?" he asked, standing.

❧

Sara glanced at Kaliska who was now staring up at her. She reached down and picked up the baby, cradling her against one hip. "Sure. Did you eat lunch?"

Istaga nodded. "I found food in the cold box."

Sara led the way down a meandering path wondering why she felt so nervous. At one point she wondered if this accommodating and solicitous Istaga was a doppelganger, and then chided herself for the thought. He didn't talk much but he smiled a lot and held her hand for a while, a gesture he'd never done before. She tried to think of things to say, aware of the silences as never before. He answered her, but the way he spoke and what he said did not sound like the Istaga she knew.

"I forgot to ask how you found me."

"John picked us up on our way into town. He dropped us here."

Sara thought of John, imagining the scene as he stopped his truck for Istaga and the baby. The man was nosy and must have pestered Istaga with questions. "What did you tell him?"

Istaga looked puzzled. "Tell?" He shook his head.

"He didn't ask you a bunch of questions?"

"No. He seemed surprised when he saw us but he didn't ask how we got here or where we'd been. He did say that you moved out here because of Raleigh. He told me what happened to Raleigh, how he died. He said it was about time the guy paid for what he had done."

The rest of the walk was made in silence with Sara gulping air every so often when she realized she was holding her breath. Istaga moved like a cat along the trail, his boot clad feet hardly making a sound. In contrast she felt heavy and cumbersome, her footsteps loud in her ears. When she stumbled over a root Istaga caught her before she went down, his awareness of her unnerving. In the past he'd always ignored her when they walked together, his gaze going into the distance like a hunter. He let go of her hand and took the baby and hoisted her up onto his shoulders. Behind her she heard him murmuring and Kaliska's giggles in response. Who was this man?

It was later in the afternoon when Sara realized that Kaliska's birthday was the following day. "We have to have a party for her," she said after explaining this very human event.

Istaga looked up from where he was puzzling over a nature magazine, trying to read the words. "A party. She will not care."

"I know, but I care and it'll be fun—a combination celebration for your return and her birthday. I'm going to run into town and get a cake and see if Rosie will join us. Is that all right with you?"

"I like Rosie."

When she met his gaze the look in his eyes was not one she recognized. Those yellow eyes were calm, placid even. She did not see even a remnant of the coyote side of him. She looked quickly away, aware of a creeping nervousness.

She was on the way to the car when Istaga called out, "Do you need anything done while you are gone?"

Sara stopped and turned, utterly surprised by the question. She shook her head. "Just make sure Kaliska doesn't hurt herself—but you already know that."

Istaga nodded and waved before turning to pick up the baby.

≈୨ৡୡ

"I know it's silly, Rosie, but he isn't the Istaga I know." Sara crossed her arms over her protruding belly, fear coiling through her stomach as she paced.

Rosie dried her hands on a towel and placed the dish of beans she'd prepared into the oven before turning to face her. "So what you're telling me is," she said, ticking the things off with her fingers, "he's considerate, he cares for the baby, he makes food and cleans up, he asked if he could help out while you were gone, and held your hand while you were on a walk together. And this bothers you?"

"He's plenty nice, that's not the problem. I just don't know this version of him."

Rosie laughed. "I'd say enjoy it while you can."

"I'm serious. How would you like it if Ben completely changed?"

"If he changed into better Ben I'd be happy about it."

Sara stared out the window. "It's hard to get used to this sanitized version, that's all."

"Didn't you say he's been living on the rez? Maybe he's changed because of that. And he's probably on his best behavior trying to win you back."

Sara let out a long sigh, trying to let go of her nerves. "Will you come tomorrow?"

"Are you kidding? Of course I'll come!"

❧

On the way home Sara thought about her reactions, wondering what was wrong with her. Why couldn't she just be happy that Istaga had become more thoughtful? She had a queer feeling in the pit of her stomach, which increased as she got closer to the trailer. She didn't know this man. Even the way he made love had changed. Her mind went to the crazy sex they had, the wildness that always accompanied their coupling. Last night's lovemaking had been sedate in comparison, with Istaga seeming worried that he might hurt her or something. Of course that could be worry about the coming baby, but when she thought back to her first pregnancy, he had not behaved this way. It hadn't mattered to him if they were in the fields, or in the cave, he'd taken her with his usual wild enthusiasm, even when she was big with child.

When she parked the car Istaga was working in the garden, weeding around her lettuces and small herbs. He looked up and hurried over as she slid out of the car and reached for her grocery bag.

"Do you need help?"

"No thanks. It's only the one. Rosie said she would come," she added, hurrying inside. She put her things away with her back to him, trying to maintain calm. When she felt his hand on her shoulder she jumped.

"What is wrong, Sara?"

She opened her mouth, trying to find words and then registered the absence of Kaliska. "Where's Kaliska?"

Istaga pointed toward the bed. "She's asleep. If you wish to talk, now is a good time."

"*You* want to talk?" She stared at him.

He grinned. "I know this is what humans do when they have been apart."

He went to the tiny living room and sat on the loveseat, watching her expectantly. "I've done everything I can to make you happy but you do not seem happy."

Sara sat next to him. "Istaga, I don't know this version of you. I don't know what to expect because you're so different from the man I knew before."

Istaga frowned. "I thought you would like me this way. I have watched the humans and how they behave together and have practiced the right things to say."

"I don't want you to fake it, Istaga. I want the real you, the one who blows up and storms around and swears."

Istaga looked confused, his eyebrows pulling together. "But you did not like that Istaga. It is that Istaga who killed a man."

"I've forgiven you for that—I know you did it for me. I've thought a lot about us while you've been gone."

"I have thought a lot, too. I have not shifted. I didn't want the wild part of me to come out again."

Sara touched his arm. "I love the wild part of you. If I had wanted a normal man I wouldn't have gotten involved with you in the first place."

Istaga stared at her. "I do not understand. I am willing to live here with you as long as I can sleep outside. Is this not enough?"

At that moment the baby gave a loud wail and both of them jumped. Sara reached her first and scooped her up from the floor where she'd fallen, but Kaliska twisted in her arms, reaching for Istaga. Sara handed her over. "Guess she feels more comfortable with you. Has she been shifting?"

Istaga soothed the baby, murmuring to her as he held her close. "Only when she's afraid."

"I wish we could have brought her up together this past year."

"But we're together now and I have learned the

ways of humans. She is still a baby in human years. Toh Yah explained that we would die sooner if we remained coyotes. I would rather live longer and be with you."

Sara nodded and then smiled. "That's a very good point, but it doesn't mean you can never shift."

"This I know, but I have no wish to hunt, so why would I?"

"Because at heart you are Coyote. Don't you miss running on four legs and your senses being so much sharper?"

Istaga stared out the window, his eyes turning dark. "I have a feeling here when you say that," he answered, his hand going to his middle belly. "But this is what I try to ignore."

"You're repressing your true nature, Istaga. It's bad to do that."

Istaga frowned, his gaze meeting hers. "Good—bad—how am I to figure it out? You make me loco," he said, shaking his head. He handed her the baby and a moment later he was out the door. By the time she hurried after him he'd disappeared. When the unmistakable howl of a coyote split the silence Kaliska squirmed, trying to get down, but Sara held her firmly. "Oh no you don't." She closed the door and locked it.

33

*C*oyote ran through the brush, aware that there were houses close by. He could smell food cooking and the human scents of soap and sweat that he'd grown used to over the months. But here there were other smells that made him want to gag, sweet and cloying, the chemicals they used to clean and bathe with.

He crouched down and slunk along, careful not to be seen before he hurtled across a road and into a field of cactus beyond. He had no idea where he was going, only that he had to get away.

The glitter of tiny points of light in the night sky brought him to a stop. He had traveled far from his mate and pup. This was wilderness that he recognized. He was unused to this shape and had to reacquaint to the stronger senses, the ability to see far into the darkness, to run on four instead of two legs. A rabbit hopped in the field ahead and he went after it, all his instincts telling him to kill and eat.

It was sometime in the night that he woke to find himself in human shape. He could still smell the blood and see the carcass of the animal he'd devoured before falling asleep. He waited for the familiar nausea, the retching that always followed, but nothing happened. It was only when he thought of Sara that his stomach clenched, but still he managed to keep the food down.

He sat in the dark and tried to puzzle out what she'd told him, but every time he turned his mind to the conversation, a fog would enter his head. He'd been so sure of himself before her pronouncement that what he was doing was bad—that word again, the one that puzzled him the most. He had not intended to be good or bad, but his attempt to make her happy had turned into another perplexing misunderstanding. Toh Yah had explained how humans did not understand one another, especially men and women whose thoughts often ran on different tracks. He puzzled about what this meant, visualizing two different paths leading through a forest, Sara on one and him on the other. How could they be together if they traveled different trails?

He let out a loud cry that didn't sound human and curled into a ball to stop the pains in his lower belly. This feeling was too familiar and what it meant was that he and Sara could not be together.

❧

Istaga wandered through a forest of pine trees, tears coursing down his cheeks. He didn't know how long he'd been gone from Black Base or even where he was. When he saw Raven flying above him he stopped. "I need your advice," he called out, but the bird kept going as though Istaga was just an ordinary human who couldn't communicate with birds. Had he become so humanized that he could no longer commune with natural life all around him? That couldn't be true since the tribe were all very much in touch with this part of their nature. They had totems and spirits they communed with on a regular basis. "What is wrong with me?" he cried out, looking at the sky.

"There is nothing wrong with you," a man's voice answered.

Istaga turned to see Toh Yah beneath the trees. "Where did you come from?"

"I told you if you needed me I'd be there. I'd say you need me right now."

Istaga nodded and wiped at his eyes. "I cannot get along with her. She has a way of making me crazy."

Toh Yah laughed. "The best ones always do," he answered. "You are trying too hard, Istaga. And she is carrying a child, which makes her more sensitive than usual."

"I don't know what she wants from me! I have tried to make her happy but nothing works."

"You've changed and she's changed. You need to get to know one another again."

"She wants me to be like I was, but that Istaga is gone."

Toh Yah met his gaze. "You are still Coyote. Don't forget that. Even though you haven't shifted much doesn't mean he isn't still inside you. I think she's missing that part of you."

"She did not like how I was as Coyote."

"Sara was upset about many things when you parted ways. Her mind was confused and she blamed you for things that were not your fault. Remember what I told you about mothers and their babies. Kaliska was gone and Sara was grieving. Making a fresh start will take time. When this new baby comes you will have another set of problems to deal with. Nothing stays the same. Go home and try again."

Home. The word conjured something that was not the place Sara lived. But it also wasn't the wilderness where they'd spent time, nor was it the rez. "I don't know where home is," Istaga muttered, staring into the distance.

"You and Sara will discover it together."

When Istaga turned to answer Toh Yah was gone.

34

"*He*'s gone walkabout!" Sara yelled into her cell phone. "He's been gone for four days now—what am I supposed to do, Rosie? I have Kaliska and I have to go to work!"

"Sara, calm down. I'm not working this week; I'll come over and watch her. But I'd suggest you cut your hours. It's getting close to your due date."

"It's still more than two months away. I thought I could manage things, but now…"

"So tell me what you said that pissed him off this time."

"Why do you always take his side?"

Rosie chuckled. "Because I know you? It's obvious how hard he was trying. Tell me what happened."

"I just told him he was repressing his true nature. It's true, Rosie—he was!"

"And he took off?"

"He said I was making him loco and then he left. I heard him howl so I assume he shifted. Kaliska's been weird since he left, always looking out the door. She's sad."

"Once he's sorted through all this he'll be back. But I'm sorry we didn't get a chance to have the party."

❧

As soon as Rosie arrived at the trailer Sara left for work. She was a nervous wreck wondering where Istaga had gone and if or when he would be back. At the moment she wished she had a therapist to call, but on second thought asking about how to get her shape shifting boyfriend to embrace his coyote side didn't sound like something a therapist would appreciate.

Joe looked up from the stove when she walked in, his face red. "Why are you always late when we're slammed, Sara? Could you take these plates out?"

Sara pulled on her apron and headed into the front room.

❧

It was five o'clock before she got home, gratified to see Rosie and Kaliska playing out in the front yard. Rosie had hung a swing from a limb of the palo verde and was pushing her in the little closed in canvas seat. Kaliska loved it, her screams of joy lifting into the still evening. "Where'd you find that?" Sara asked.

"It belongs to a friend of mine whose baby has outgrown it. Kaliska and I took a little ride and picked it up. How was work?"

"Tiring. I think you might be right about cutting my hours. My legs are killing me. I need a beer. Do you want one?"

"Sure, but I've got to go soon. Ben's coming down."

Sara went inside and grabbed a couple of beers from the refrigerator and hurried outside again. "So tell me how that came about," she asked.

Rosie reached for the bottle Sara held out. "He called and said we needed to talk. Don't know what to expect, but I'm hoping we can figure something out." She tipped the bottle up and then gave Kaliska another push.

Sara sat in one of the plastic chairs she'd purchased for the party that never happened. "Wish Istaga would come by and tell me we need to talk. I'm willing to do just about anything to keep him here."

"Really? Last I heard you weren't happy with him at all. What's changed?"

Sara pressed her lips together. "I guess thinking about how unfair I've been. It was what you said about him being on his best behavior that got me. He'd been here less than twenty-four hours before I chased him away again. When will I learn?"

Rose smiled. "Maybe you just did. Remember this the next time you find yourself getting on his case about something."

"If there is a next time," Sara muttered, taking a long swig from her bottle. "If I wasn't nearly seven months pregnant I'd go and look for him."

Rosie laughed. "Unless you shift I can't see it, Sara."

Sara stared at her friend. "That's a great idea. Can you keep the baby tonight?"

"You can't be serious! I thought you couldn't shift anymore."

"I did it when Raleigh almost got Kaliska. I can do it if I care enough. And right now all I care about is finding him. I can't believe how sweet he was and how

I just shut him down. He must be going through hell right now!"

"You do know it's hunting season again?"

Sara frowned. "I thought it ended in January."

"Not this kind of hunting. There don't seem to be any restrictions at all—I was sure you knew this."

"I must have forgotten. That means Istaga's in danger."

"It also means that you and your unborn child will be in danger. This is a very bad idea."

"Please, Rosie. I'll call and leave a message for Joe that I'm not feeling well. He has a gal he calls when I'm not there."

Rosie shook her head. "I hope you know what you're doing."

&

When Rosie left for home a half hour later she had Kaliska with her. As soon as the car was out of sight Sara hurried down a twisting trail that connected with the wilderness between town and the mountains. Once she got a good distance away from the roads and cars she shifted and ran for the foothills.

It was hard going, her belly big with the pup, her stamina not what it should be. She had to rest several times, her thoughts confused about what her purpose here was. But something drove her on even when she heard the shots being fired in the distance. This signified danger but in her coyote mind there was something more important that kept her going.

35

$\mathcal{I}$t was deep in the night when Istaga finally reached the trailer. He knocked and waited and then knocked again. When there was no answer he searched under the flowerpot where he knew Sara kept an extra key and let himself inside. There was no one there. Frantic he hurried outside, surprised to see Sara's mechanical beast still parked in the driveway. Where could they be?

He shifted to take a whiff of the area around. And that's when he picked up the unmistakable scent of his mate. He took off down the trail.

The moon was up, lighting the way and casting shadows that swayed and changed every time a cloud went by. Coyote dodged cactus and brush as he hurtled toward the shots being fired in the distance. This was dangerous but this was where the scent was leading him. With his sharp vision he could see the humans with their sticks that spewed fire in the distance and knew exactly who they were. No normal hunters came out in the middle of the night to shoot at coyotes. He heard the yips but couldn't tell if it was the hunters calling the coyotes or if this was a real coyote trying to warn their pack. He kept going, keeping out of sight as best he could.

He lost the scent for a while but then picked it up

again. She was headed into the midst of these humans and there was nothing he could do but follow her. When a loud crack split the air he huddled behind a bush, his hackles raised in alarm. And that was when he heard his mate call, her howl of pain pushing adrenaline into his veins. He took off in that direction.

They hunters were all around him, he could hear their mumbled conversations as he crept through the tall grass. Another crack came, making him cringe. He saw one of them drag a coyote out from under some brush, straining to see if it was his mate. From the way it hung from the man's hands it was very dead. Coyote stopped the howl that was about to come out of his mouth and skirted around the group and found his mate's scent again. She was still alive and she wasn't far.

When he found her she was huddled under a spiny bush. There was blood on her fur and her eyes were wide with terror. He nosed her and crept close before he shifted. "Sara? Have you been shot?"

She looked at him and a second later she was a human woman trembling in a light denim shirt that barely covered her enormous belly. She clutched her stomach. "They shot me," she gasped. "The baby is coming."

Istaga picked her up in his arms and ran.

36

Sara was dimly aware of what was going on. She remembered running across a field in search of Istaga and then the sound of gunshots. A second after that she collapsed and crawled to a place of safety. As a coyote she wasn't aware of the pain as much as the fear of being found. But now white-hot agony seared through her body and with it the excruciating cramping of labor. She gasped and clenched her teeth as her body jolted against Istaga's chest as he ran. If the baby came now she wasn't at all sure it would survive. But he was coming and then the searing hot pain had her gasping and retching, her hands going to her belly. When she brought them up again they were covered in dark blood. When she tried to say something to Istaga her words where lost, the sound of his labored breathing blotting them out.

The pain was intolerable and she tried not to cry out every time it came over her, but finally she felt the blackness descend and wondered fleetingly if this was it. A deep sadness went through her as she let go of consciousness.

When she opened her eyes again she could see the lights of Black Base in the distance. She was still alive and somehow Istaga had known where to take her, the bright lights of the emergency room assaulting her vision as he ran toward the hospital. Sara had no idea how much time had gone by, only that she might live after all. Now if only the baby was safe too.

Istaga shouted something to one of the orderlies and then she was on a gurney and being quickly wheeled away.

≪≫

Istaga pushed away the almost overwhelming urge to howl. He'd watched the night turn into day as he paced up and down the stench-filled room, waiting for some word about Sara. The sun was high now and still he was here wondering if she was alive or dead. There were others here, their looks wary as they watched him. He knew they were afraid, that his expression was more animal than human. At least he'd resisted the urge to shift. He glanced down at his blood-soaked shirt and jeans, the dark stains where it had dried. The smell of it made him want to retch. She had lost too much of this. He resumed his pacing, his fists clenching and unclenching as he imagined the worst.

"Is there an Istaga here?"

He glanced at the woman in white standing in the doorway. "I am Istaga," he said.

"Come with me."

He couldn't form words to ask what was happening as he followed her down a hallway and then through a swinging door. She led him to a curtained off area and held one section open. "Your wife is here," she said.

Istaga stumbled into the space, his gaze going to

the still form on the bed. "Sara?" He reached her in one stride and took the hand she held out. "Are you all right?"

Sara smiled wanly. "I think so. They got the bullet out. But how is the baby?"

Istaga shook his head.

Sara tried to push herself up and then slumped back, her face contorting in agony. "You have to find out," she pleaded, squeezing his hand.

Istaga looked around. "How do I do that?"

"You go out there and ask the first person in a white coat that you come to. Please, Istaga."

Istaga let go of her hand and hurried beyond the curtain. A woman with a white coat was standing there with a clipboard. "Is my pup alive?" he asked her.

She looked up, her gaze meeting his. "Pup? Where did you come from?"

"My mate is there," he said, pointing, toward the curtain. "The hunters hurt her. But she was pregnant. Is the baby…?"

The nurse looked toward the curtain and seemed to register what was going on. She took hold of his arm. "No need for alarm, Mr. Istaga," she said. "The baby is in the nursery. He was premature and needs some special care."

"He is alive?"

"Yes. He'll be fine."

"Sara, my mate, wishes to see him."

"We'll get him to her as fast as we can. Luckily he was a big baby and quite developed for being so premature. He's a strong one." She smiled and then turned back to her clipboard.

Istaga hurried behind the curtain to give her the news but Sara had fallen asleep. He pulled up a chair and waited, holding her hand while she slept. His mind was full of the sounds of the night before, the hunters, the calls of coyotes, the terrible feeling in his chest when he found her under the tree. Tears welled and he brushed them away.

The trip he'd made was a haze, the only thing in his mind to take her to the place where she could find help. He hadn't known where he was going or even how long it took to get there. All he wanted now was to curl up next to her and hold her close.

❦

When Sara woke Istaga was in a chair next to the bed. As soon as she opened her eyes he leaned close. "The pup is fine."

"When will they bring him?"

"He is a word that I cannot remember."

"Premature?"

"That is it. The woman said he is strong."

Sara felt her entire body relax. She pulled Istaga close and kissed him. "You saved my life," she whispered. When he tried to crawl into the bed with her she pushed him back. "There isn't room for both of us in here."

"Where did you get hurt?" he asked, pulling back the covers.

Sara pulled the gown back to show him the red gash where the doctor had removed the bullet from her side. "Any further and it might have killed him," she said, pulling her gown down as the doctor arrived.

"So, Mrs. Istaga, you had a very close call. Let's take a look, shall we?"

When the doc lifted her gown Sara met Istaga's narrowed gaze over his shoulder. She shook her head and frowned when she saw the feral protective expression that came into his eyes, the curled up lip that revealed his canines. For a second he looked all animal. But as soon as the doctor pulled up the covers and wrote something on his clipboard Istaga relaxed.

"If that bullet had been one inch to the left you would have lost your baby. As it is he is a strong and healthy newborn despite being a month early. If you would like to feed him the nurses can bring him in now."

"I would love to feed him," Sara answered. "But just to let you know, my baby was two months early, not one."

The doc turned on his way out. "That is quite impossible, Mrs. Istaga. No seven-month-old baby is that developed."

"He has an unusual father," she said, slanting a glance at Istaga.

"Maybe you had your dates wrong," he said, and then he was through the curtain and on to his next patient.

"Are you sure he's mine?" Istaga asked, looking worried.

Sara laughed. "He's either yours or he was implanted in my belly by the gods. You are the only man I've had sex with since we met over three years ago."

It was twenty minutes later that the nurse arrived with the baby. Istaga helped Sara sit up and then the nurse placed the bundle in her arms. She looked down on him for the first time with Istaga standing next to her. "Do you still think he's another man's baby?" she asked, glancing up. The baby was dark-haired, the look on his face startlingly familiar. Even being this new it was very apparent who his father was.

"But his eyes are not my color."

"They will be," Sara said, opening her gown.

Sara spent two nights in the hospital before they allowed her to leave. They told her they were worried about infection and also wanted to monitor the baby. Istaga refused to leave her side except when she insisted that he find someone to call Rosie to let her know what had happened.

"She has Kaliska and I'm sure she's worried sick," she told him, shooing him out of the room.

After the nurses made their nighttime rounds Istaga crawled into bed with her, one arm wrapped around her middle as he snuggled close. They had brought in a bassinet for the baby so that she could feed him in the night. When he cried Istaga was there to lift him out and hand him to her. Between the feedings Sara slept better than she had in a very long time.

On the morning of the third day Rosie arrived with Kaliska, breezing into the room as though she belonged there. She said hello to Istaga, handed Kaliska over and then went to take a look at the new baby. "No question who his father is," she said, turning to smile at Istaga. She pulled out a chair and sat on the other side of the bed next to Sara. "Now, can you tell me what exactly what happened? The nurse said something about an accident that brought on labor."

"Sara was shot," Istaga said, placing a kiss on the top of his daughter's head.

"Istaga saved my life," Sara added.

Rosie looked from one to the other. "Were you a coyote when you got shot?" she whispered.

Sara nodded. "It was the hunters, Rosie. I thought all the protests against them had done something, but apparently they didn't."

Rosie smiled, a gleam in her brown eyes. "They have now. The news has been full of a woman who was shot and nearly killed during this latest hunt. I had no idea it was you. You may have inadvertently put a stop to the entire thing."

37

It had been a month and a half since Sara and Istaga brought the baby home to the trailer. Sara was gradually settling into the routine of two children, very thankful to have Istaga to help. But it was becoming abundantly clear that the trailer was too small.

"Should I get a job?" Istaga asked, turning from where he was preparing food for Kaliska.

Sara smiled. "I think we'll manage. Thanks to Joe's kindness I have paid maternity leave from my job." So far Istaga had been more help than she ever expected, her earlier worries of not knowing who he was gone as soon as he carried her all the way to the hospital. Without him she'd be dead and the baby too. He was more like his old self now, anger sometimes getting the best of him, his use of four-letter words back. But his kindness and care for the two children was a new phenomenon that she appreciated more than she could say.

"I can do many things now," he continued. "I learned while I was with Toh Yah."

"I wish we had the money to build a house. This place gets smaller every day. Four people are not supposed to live in such a small space."

"I can build a house."

"You may be able to build one but we don't have

the money to buy the materials or the land to put it on."

Istaga looked hopeful. "In the forest?"

"We would at least need a water supply, Istaga, and if we cut down trees and built in the BLM wilderness we'd get caught and put in jail."

"It seems that many things cause this punishment."

"There are laws that can't be broken. Coyotes have them too, just not the same." The baby began his mewling cry and she sat down to feed him, unwrapping the sling she used to carry him around. "What are we going to name the little guy?" she asked, looking up. "We have to think of something strong since he brought us back together." She looked down at the dark head at her breast, a wave of love moving through her.

"Cheveyo means spirit warrior."

"How do you know that?"

"It is one of the Navajo words Toh Yah taught me. He said if we had a boy it would be a good name for him."

"He knew I was pregnant?"

Istaga shook his head. "He didn't say he did. But I would not be surprised. He appeared to me many times over the past months before I made it up to Page. He seems to know things before they happen."

Sara laughed. "I do remember that about him. Do the Natives have a naming ceremony for their children?"

Istaga nodded and then placed a bowl of mashed squash and sweet potato in front of Kaliska. She was propped on pillows in front of the tiny counter. "I have participated in this ceremony. Toh Yah can do it for us if you decide it is the right thing."

"I like the name. It seems like what he is—part coyote and part human. When do you think he'll shift?"

"He will not shift unless we do, Sara. We can raise him as human."

"But you'll want to shift once in a while and I...well, I do enjoy it occasionally," she added, her mind going to the times she and Coyote hunted together and her early experiences when Kaliska was first born. There was something freeing about it, even though she preferred her human life.

Istaga shrugged. "It is up to you."

"And what about Kaliska? He'll learn how to shift from her."

"Maybe he will."

When Istaga turned his back to help Kaliska with her food, Sara wondered why he was leaving it up to her. There were still times like these when she felt she didn't know him, but his changeable ways also excited her. Her breath caught as she imagined him without clothes.

❧

Both babies were asleep when Sara pressed close to Istaga. He turned to face her in the bed, his eyes dark. "You are not healed," he said.

"I'm fine," she said. "It's been more than a full turning of the moon."

"Sara, we have not spoken about our

misunderstandings."

Misunderstandings, a new word he'd added to his increasing vocabulary. "You mean everything that happened before? I was hoping we could move on. We've both changed and we're getting to know each other again."

"I thought you would want to talk about it."

"Not any more. I just want to connect. It's been a long time."

Istaga watched her for a while before he traced the side of her face with his fingers. "I'm afraid, Sara. I cannot leave you again." He glanced toward the two sleeping babies.

"I don't want you to ever leave. If we argue it won't lead to that, I promise." She put her hand on his bare chest, feeling his heart beating under her fingers. She couldn't believe she was begging him to make love with her, but at this moment she could barely contain herself. "Please, Istaga."

His expression didn't change but she could tell he was holding himself back. He looked away and let out a sigh. When he turned back one side of his mouth quirked, indicating that he understood the irony of what was going on here.

"Before we mate you must promise you will never use the words 'good' or 'bad' about something I've done or not done—those words are used when humans speak to dogs. If you are angry you need to explain why instead of blaming me for it all."

"Will you promise not to kill anyone else?"

Istaga stared at her silently until she finally said,

"Okay, okay. I promise."

The quirking turned into a grin and then he laughed. Before she could say anything else he'd pulled her close. She felt his teeth on her neck, nipping and making chills go down her spine. When his mouth moved towards hers she closed her eyes meeting him halfway. Their tongues met and clung, his hands working their usual magic. And then they were together in some faraway place where sensation was all that mattered. Shadows danced, the sound of flute music adding to the dream-like atmosphere. This was what she remembered—this was how it was supposed to be.

Epilogue

$\mathcal{B}$aby Cheveyo was three months old before they were able to organize a naming ceremony. Toh Yah arrived from Page in an old truck that he referred to his 'pony', with Haseya in the passenger seat. Ben arrived with Rosie, and from the look in Rosie's eyes it was obvious they had come to some sort of arrangement that both agreed on.

They held the festivities near the mountains in a sacred grove of pine trees that Toh Yah knew about. Raven was there, swooping and soaring in the clear sky above them, his cawing distinctively joyful. Kaliska shifted a couple of times just for the thrill of it, eventually kneeling next to her little brother and kissing him over and over.

After the chanting and the burning of sage, and each person bestowing their love upon the newly named child of the universe, they all went to the Desert Café. Joe had prepared a buffet, closing the restaurant to accommodate their party. It was the least he could do after everything they'd been through, he told them, laying out the platters of vegetables, meats and cheeses and pouring the champagne.

He pulled Sara aside at one point and assured her that he would continue her benefits for another couple of weeks if she promised to come back to work. By now she'd confessed to her alias, explaining the need for it because of Raleigh and his blackmail. "So is this all of it now?" Joe had asked, his lips curling up in a smile.

A week later Rosie brought the news that Raleigh's death and the near death of a pregnant woman shot by hunters sparked a flurry of letters to the editor. There was outrage and the threat of lawsuits to Fish and Game as well as the Predator Masters organization. Hunting in this area was put on hold until they could sort out a new set of rules. Apparently Rosie had followed through with her twitter account, @truthbetold, adding fuel to the already burning fire.

But the best news of all came a month later when John passed along a letter that had finally made its way to him after going to Sara's former rental address. It was Rosie who brought it to the trailer one evening, saying that she hoped they had a beer to give her for her troubles.

It was from a lawyer in Duluth and revealed the unexpected revelation that Sara would inherit Raleigh's entire estate, which was sizable. It was still in probate since Raleigh had not left a will, but the bulk sum would come to her in a few months' time. It was nearly two million dollars.

After that news Sara shared her dream of a house that would accommodate Coyote's needs as well as hers—the log cabin with the French doors she'd imagined months before. When Istaga suggested they find some land up on the rez close to Toh Yah Sara agreed.

"I will build it," he told her solemnly. And then he pulled her close and kissed her.

####

If you liked this book please leave a review! And don't forget to sign up for advance notice of deals and freebies!

Goto

http://forms.aweber.com/form/31/557871031.htm)

for sign-up sheet:

About the author

Nikki Broadwell lives in Tucson, Arizona, at the base of the Catalina Mountains with her husband of over thirty years, a standard poodle and a cat.

Coyote Sunrise is her eleventh novel and follows *Just Another Desert Sunset* in storyline and setting, taking place in the desert landscape that has become her home.

Nikki's e-mail: nikkibroadwell@comcast.net
Website: www.wolfmoontrilogy.com

Other books by Nikki:

Just Another Desert Sunset (first of the shapeshifting series)

Wolfmoon Trilogy:
The *Moonstone*
Saille, the Willow
The Wolf Moon
Bridge of Mist and Fog—sequel to Wolfmoon Trilogy

Gypsy Series:
Gypsy's Quest
Gypsy's Return
Gypsy's Secret

Summer McCloud paranormal series:
Murder in Plain Sight
Saffron and Seaweed

To reach Nikki: nikkibroadwell@comcast.net
www.wolfmoontrilogy.com

Made in the USA
Charleston, SC
15 January 2016